George Augustus Sala

The Baddington Peerage

Who won, and who wore it. A story of the best and the worst society. Vol. 3

George Augustus Sala

The Baddington Peerage
Who won, and who wore it. A story of the best and the worst society. Vol. 3

ISBN/EAN: 9783337411343

Printed in Europe, USA, Canada, Australia, Japan

Cover: Foto ©Andreas Hilbeck / pixelio.de

More available books at **www.hansebooks.com**

The Baddington Peerage:

Who won, and who wore it.

A Story of the Best and the Worst Society.

BY

George Augustus Sala,

Author of

" *Twice Round the Clock*," " *Lady Chesterfield's Letters to her Daughter*,"
" *A Journey Due North*," " *Gaslight and Daylight*,"
&c., &c., &c.

In Three Volumes.

Vol. III.

London:
Charles J. Skeet, King William Street, Strand.
1860.

CONTENTS OF VOLUME III.

CHAP. XXXV. PAGE.

CONTAINS THE PARTICULARS OF ANOTHER

WEDDING 1

CHAP. XXXVI.

HOW LORD BADDINGTON KEPT HIS PROMISE . 11

CHAP. XXXVII.

A HAPPY MARRIAGE 24

CHAP. XXXVIII.

BEFORE THE BALL 50

CHAP. XXXIX.

THE BALL 66

CHAP. XL.

PAGE.

RUN TO EARTH 78

CHAP. XLI.

LORD BADDINGTON SUPS AND BREAKFASTS . 97

CHAP. XLII.

EIGHTEEN HUNDRED AND FORTY-FIVE . . 111

CHAP. XLIII.

TO PARISH CLERKS AND OTHERS . . . 130

CHAP. XLIV.

HER GRACE 153

CHAP. XLV.

THE DUCHESS OF MINNIVER RECEIVES A
DISTINGUISHED CIRCLE . . . 173

CHAP. XLVI.

MR. TINCTOP SPEAKS HIS MIND . . . 188

CHAP. XLVII.

THE ELEVENTH HOUR 207

CHAP. XLVIII.   PAGE.

WHITHER TEND THE CROOKED ROADS .   225

CHAP. XLIX.

SHADOWS 242

THE BADDINGTON PEERAGE.

CHAP. XXXV.

CONTAINS THE PARTICULARS OF ANOTHER WEDDING.

THE readers of this story, I am convinced, must, as far as a very great majority of them are concerned, personally detest me, the writer of the " Baddington Peerage." For I at once acknowledge, and am willing to do penance for the offence: I know full well that I stand in direct contradistinction to those writers of serial romances who possess the faculty of " knowing how to leave off at the right time."

I am perfectly aware that I always leave off at the *wrong* time; and that instead of ending a chapter with an astounding incident, or the enunciation of some mysterious proposition to be satisfactorily solved in the next published portion, I leave my readers in a state of uncomfortable suspense as to what is going to be done, or "who is meaning what"—to paraphrase a late example of English elegance of composition in a leader in the "Times" newspaper. I have my motives for this, as for most things; but, think I may as well continue the conversation between the Lord and the Lady Baddington, cut short in the last Chapter.

"I am a very young woman, my Lord," she commenced, "but I have had, perhaps, more opportunities of seeing the world than usually fall to the lot of my sex. I called you a villain, and I will tell you the reason. You did your best — you, Peer, officer, gentleman, and all the rest of it — you tried your hardest to ruin that poor little dancing girl."

"'Pon my word—" the Peer began in half stupid remonstrance.

" Just hear me out," his grandaunt resumed. " I daresay I am prosing, and, as you men call it, boring you: but at the same time it may do you a little good to listen to what I have to say. You met the poor child in Liverpool, and filled her silly head with a notion that she was to become your wife. She was to be your wife. She was to be a lady. A lady forsooth! All your arts, all your devices, all your cunning wiles, were put in force for the miserable purpose of calling that girl your own. By the mercy of God she has escaped you."

" Well, as to that — " the Nobleman interposed, curling his lip superciliously the while.

" Say that again if you dare," exclaimed the Woman — she *was* a woman, every inch of her — " and I will brand you as a liar as well as a villain. The girl is as pure as unfallen snow."

" Came away, though, from Liverpool, in a post-chaise."

" You cur, you know very well how she

came, and why she came, and how, at the
last moment, all your schemes were spoiled,
and all your hopes frustrated. She ran away
from the lodging you had taken for her
at Pentonville, Viscount Baddington — that
lodging which you vainly thought to turn
into a Capua; she ran away, because she
had discovered that the god of her idolatry
was a base fetish; that with the front of
brass there were feet of clay. She ran away,
because she had found you out. Now listen,
and leave off biting your lips. *I* had been
to the opera to hear Malibran in Fidelio —
or, stay, no, it was to hear Pasta utter her
inimitable *Io.* My dear departed husband
left me in the crush room — I suppose at-
tracted by the charms of some demirep,—and
when Lady Baddington's carriage stopped
the way, there was only Lady Baddington
to occupy it. But, coming out, I saw crouching
at the base of one of the pillars of the Opera
Colonnade a little trembling form, that seemed
strangely out of place in *that* colonnade. *You*
know the ladies who frequent the place,

Viscount. Not the viscountesses who come out of the Opera, but the viscountesses who go into the 'Blue Posts.' I will own that I am a very odd and eccentric woman; and, something striking me in the appearance of this poor little child clinging round the column, I took her at once into the carriage, to question her, much to the surprise of my servants."

"I really must—" Lord Baddington tried to introduce.

"The girl was Manuelita."

"By Jove!"

"She told me the whole story: told it me with hysterical sobbings and moanings, and almost inarticulate fragments of speech. Do you know what she would have done if I had not so discovered her—if I had not, wearer of a coronet as I am, been odd and eccentric enough to put a poor forlorn outcast into my grand chariot? She would have drowned herself. Every week, Charles Falcon, there are scores and scores of wretched things such as these, who find their bed in the waters, and pillow their heads under the tide. And most of them are not so happy as Manuelita. Most of them are lost, lost, lost, to everything in this world; but to receive, I believe and hope, the supreme kind commiserating forgiveness in the next. Dissolute man, think and tremble! Think of the ocean of tears, think of the abyss of unutterable woe—all caused by the indulgence of a momentary whim!"

She stood up saying this, her finger pointing out—the Cassandra of her sex. I wonder whether she meant what she said! Was Sterne sincere when he wrote about the prisoner, and Maria, and the recording angel, and dying Lieutenant .

And she immediately became Lady Baddington again.

"The end of all which is, my Lord, that I want you to promise me, on your solemn word and honour, as a nobleman and a gentleman, that you will never by word or deed, molest Manuelita again."

"The doose of it is—I beg pardon, your

Ladyship—I can't make out why you should feel such an interest in the little party."

" I have my own reasons, my Lord. Will you make me the promise?"

" Too happy, I'm sure "

" Only mind and keep your word. I will illustrate my meaning by a little story, just as the people who write in the newspapers begin their leading articles with a stale and hackneyed anecdote."

She knew everything, this woman. To use a very vulgar expression, she was "up to every move on the board." She could not have known, of course, what she did, if the druggist in Drury Lane had not had the right to call her " Polly."

" Once upon a time," she went on, settling her muslins, and shaking her golden hair, "an officer in the Guards was travelling by the express night-train to Southampton. In the same first-class carriage there was a lady, very young and very handsome, and I am afraid that before they reached Winchester—(there were no other persons in the carriage)—she

permitted this bold young guardsman to im-
print one kiss—he gave, and she allowed
no more—upon her gloved hand. It was a
freak, a caprice, a 'bit of fun,' just like the
kiss which the beautiful Duchess of Devonshire gave a sweep when Mr. Fox was being
elected for Westminster. But she made him
take a solemn oath that he would never reveal
what had taken place. It fell out that our
guardsman, about six months afterwards, did,
in the smoking-room of his club in St. James's
Street, break his oath, and with the boastful,
lying qualities, common to men, gave the story
with some additions and alterations perfectly
and wantonly false. A fortnight afterwards
he had an invitation to stay a week with a
distant relation of his—an old admiral, who
lived in a charming villa on the banks of the
river Itchen, close to Southampton. He had
never seen this relative before; but some
family matter had to be arranged, and he went
down. He was received with the most cordial
hospitality, especially by the admiral's wife,
who was very young, and very handsome, and

who, by the merest chance in the world,
turned out to be the identical lady with whom
he had travelled, per night express train from
London to Southampton.   She gave him her
hand, ungloved this time, smiled upon him
very sweetly, and just before dinner drew him
on one side, and with a sweeter smile than
ever, told him, in a discreet whisper, that if he
would come round at twelve o'clock that
night to a certain window at the back of the
house overlooking the river, and only separated
from its brink by a narrow footway, she had
something very important, and perhaps pleasant, to communicate to him.   He came
punctually at the appointed time.   The moon
was shining very brightly.   The window was
opened: and a lady in a night-dress beckoned
a tall and handsome cavalier (as the novels
say) to advance to her."

" And she let him in through the window.
By Jove, what a plucky one!"

" She said this: 'Captain Darell, you are a
liar and a traitor.' She did this; she put
a pistol to his head, right in the centre of his

forehead, between his curling locks which parted in the middle, and she blew his brains out, and Captain Darell fell into the river Itchen, and was found there next day, very wet and very dead."

" She was hanged, of course."

" Not the least in the world. She took the precaution of throwing the pistol into the river as well as the man. There was a great talk about the affair. There was adjourned inquest after adjourned inquest ; some called it murder, and some suicide; but as Captain Darell stood to lose enormously on the next Derby, and was dreadfully in debt besides, the general opinion inclined towards *felo de se*. He was buried very respectably, and the Admiral's wife wore mourning for him."

" I'll promise," said Lord Baddington.

" You had better. She was a relative of mine."

CHAP. XXXVI.

HOW THE PEER KEPT HIS PROMISE.

CARNIVAL time, and in Paris. Although
it was the last of the three *jours féries*
— the night of *Mardi Gras* — the eve of the
once famous but now degenerated and inglo-
rious *descente de la courtille* — there was less
conversation in the gay city of Paris about
the Carnival than about the cold; and men's
thoughts ran more upon Réaumur and his
thermometer than on Musard and his *bal
masqué*. It was *so* cold. So cold on the
bridges, that the blind beggars, tootling dismally on their cracked flutes and rattling their
battered tin money-boxes, had one and all
decamped; that the itinerant cake and sweetmeat sellers on the quays were to be found

nowhere. A piercing blast went along with this cold, which swept before icy gusts of little particles of frozen dust, which blew down your back and into your eyes, and made you generally miserable. The steams of *vin chaud*, or heated and spiced wine, issued from every *cabaret ;* and every café was crammed with *consommateurs.* Here also, and in the estaminets, was a tremendous vapour from the largest, most powerful, and most evil-smelling cigars, and from the blackest and most essential-oily-redolent perfume; the rattle of dominoes was incessant; the shuffling of the limp, pawn-broker's-duplicate-looking cards persistent; the shrieks of the *garçons* to intimate that they were " there " instead of being " here," where they were required to be, the growls of the customers who wanted more grogs, and more boxes of dominoes, and more newspapers, were high above the din. The Boulevards were nearly deserted by foot passengers, though the road was thronged by carriages. The *bœuf gras* and the barouches and *carrioles* — filled with maskers paid and costumed by

the police, and whose tawdry trappings, yellow-
white drapery, and painted faces, looked inexpressibly ghastly against the brilliant, heaven-
sent snow — had failed in attracting the usual
scampish crowd of sight-seers, who kept under
shelter; so the police maskers had it all their
own way. On they went, these forlorn rogues
and roguesses, a little excited by gun-powder
brandy and peppered *petit bleu*, consumed at
the barrier cabarets; on they went, forlorn
mummers, their poor noses a little pinched
and numbed by the cold; the cold-drawn tears
from their bleared, winking eyes furrowing a
little in unseemly streaks the brickdust and
bismuth on their cheeks. They were not a
good sight to look at, these fancy-ball guests
of the Rue-Jérusalem, these carnival protégés
of the prefecture; they made you shudder
rather, dreadful beings — *for you knew what
they must become when the saturnalia was over.*

And this rabble rout going by, some in close
carriages, some in open cabs, cabriolets, and
carts, shouting and yelling, and pretending to
throw sweetmeats at the passers by, which

they dared not do in reality, in consequence
of a recent ordinance of the Prefect of Police,
came out the sudden sun, and shone upon the
raggamuffins, and upon the virgin snow.

The day cleared up wonderfully before dusk;
but though the snow had ceased to fall, and
the sky was even a tender, loving blue, the
cold was still almost intolerably intense. About
four o'clock or so, some of the most inveterate
Boulevard *flâneurs* came out, wrapped up to
the nose in furs and woollens, to lounge for
half an hour between the Rue Vivienne and
the Café de la Madeleine; but the great places
of resort were the almost innumerable *passages*.

Here moved old veterans of the Imperial
Guard—the old Guard remember—in closely-
bottomed surtouts, and with tight black stocks,
and the ribbon of the Legion at their button
holes. And there were staring young *piou-
pious*, fresh from the conscription and the
drill-sergeants, wandering about with their
hands in the pockets of their baggy red
breeches, and gazing at everything, with a
stupid stare of equal amazement and admira-

tion. And there were gay officers, with shining bullion epaulettes, aiguillettes, embroidery,
crosses and ribbons, plumes, trailing sabres,
and clanking spurs; Parisian exquisites of the
first water, elegantly swaddled in broad-cloth
pelisses, lined and trimmed with rich furs; —
and there were ladies in mantles, and cloaks,
and pelisses, and capes, likewise furred and
velveted, and who were otherwise attired with
delicious and tasteful elegance, and wore
bonnets of ravishing form on their heads; who
were *bien gantées, bien chaussées,* and *bien
lacées;* — but woe is me for the lowering
brows, the high cheekbones, the noses too
much *retroussés,* or else sinking in the opposite
extreme, and standing out in arrogant aqui-
linity, like the prow of a Roman galley; the
thin lips, the discoloured teeth, the coarse and
often art-improved complexions. No! no! no!
Witty if you please, accomplished if you please,
fascinating without a doubt, graceful beyond
compare; but beauteous, no! I could count
the fair women of France on the keys of a
pianoforte, and carry them on my back up all the
steps of the Monument, without taking breath.

So, at least, thought Philip Leslie, who, wrapped up in a stout overcoat, walked moodily from passage to passage, with his arm in that of his "friend" Doctor Ionides, in the vain attempt to dispel some portion of the gloomy and bitter feelings which hung over him like a pall. The Doctor was in high spirits, and in an astonishing "carrick" of apple-green cloth — an article strongly resembling the "Benjamin" which our hackney-coachmen and night-watchmen were formerly accustomed to wear—which said "carrick" was profusely braided; and decorated, in addition, with collars, cuffs, and trimming of costly sable, looked most imposingly wintry. The flaxen beard, and flowing hair of the Doctor, luxuriant as it was bright in colour, and the large green spectacles that he wore, gave him moreover a doctorial and erudite look which was very grand to see. That Doctor Ionides must have been Doctor Ionides, there cannot be the slightest doubt; but I much question whether, supposing the astute Mr. Leather-sides had been present, he would not have been in a slight state of dubiety touching

Doctor Ionides's voice, which, if truth must be told, bore a very strong resemblance to the voice of a friend of ours who once went by the name of Jachimo, Professor, but previously by that of Pollyblank, Captain.

Cum multis aliis, very probably.

"A fellow asked me at the table d'hôte yesterday," the Doctor remarked, laughingly, "how it happened, if I were a Greek, that I spoke English so well, and had such fair hair. I settled him in no time; talked to him of Sclavism and Panslavism, the Russo-Greek Church, the Eurasians of Bombay, the Jews of Honan, and the blue-eyed Affghans; told him all about the one primeval language; and he gave in, and complimented me upon my eruditipn, said he should be delighted if I would give his son, who had recently been plucked for his " little go " at Oxford, a few lessons in universal grammar, and stood a bottle of " Liebfraumilch: I'm very fond of still Hock, especially Liebfraumilch.

"You are a curious fellow," his companion responded, looking up into his face with an expression in which there was, however, far more curiosity than admiration. "You seem to know a good deal about most things. How did you manage to learn so much?"

"I beg your pardon, my artistic friend, how did you manage to learn to paint?"

"Oh! I picked it up somehow."

"And I, likewise, picked up mine some-how," Doctor Ionides complacently con-tinued, "very 'somehow,' too, it was, indeed. I believe that I have read the backs of more books than anyone alive, with the excep-tion of the man who does the cataloguing in the British Museum. For my Latin I am indebted to the hatchments on swell houses, and the scutcheons in the undertaker's shops, and the mottoes in the regimental colours in the 'Army List.' My French and geography I picked up from the guide-books and vo-cabularies on the book-stalls, and my use of the globes from having travelled about from one end of the earth to the other, backwards and forwards, for twenty years. Add to this that my father paid a great deal of money

for my schooling, and that I did really
manage to learn something while at school;
and that I have seen many men and many
cities.   The celebrated Ulysses did the same,
you may remember, and may form a definite
idea as to how the picking up process was
successfully carried out in my case."

" Then why—" The Painter hesitated.

" Go on, my friend, go on; you cannot
offend me.   Of the rhinoceros is the hide of
Doctor Ionides, and of the hippopotamus the
skin of his moral sensitiveness."

" Then, why, to be plain with you, do you
make such a villanous use of your abilities?
I don't want to flatter you, for to tell the
truth, I don't exactly like you; but you are a
clever fellow, there's no denying that!"

" My canvas-covering friend," the Doctor
composedly replied, laying his large, fur-
gloved hand on the other's shoulder, " don't
share with the tens of thousands of two-legged
donkeys—don't start, don't be offended—that
itching desire to pry into the motives of other
men.   As well may you strive to inquire why

a dog going down a street, stops as though about to turn to the right, then suddenly to the right then suddenly changing his *mind* (as if he could have a mind!) crosses the road and turns to the left. As well might you inquire why the cat is born a deadly enemy to the rat; it is all very well to say to exterminate the rat, but then why is the rat to be exterminated at all? As well may you ask why the ass should bray, or the horse should whinny suddenly after hours of dead silence. Take my advice, analyse and scan your motives and let other men's motives be. Can you understand any man? Can you understand the man we used to read about at school, Sylla? Can you understand why Baron should have been a bribe-taker, or the Duke of Marlborough the robber of soldier's pence? But, by the way, my friend, may I ask you whether *you* are making the best use of your abilities?"

" I — I" stammered the Painter. " Well, well — I have always earned my living honestly—honourably."

" Is it earning it honestly — honourably —
to be here in Paris, kicking about the Passage
Colbert, and spending the money lent to you
by the Right Honourable Viscountess Baddington ?"

" The money is all advanced to me on
account of pictures 1 am commissioned to
paint for her Ladyship," the Painter cried
out indignantly, but blushing suspiciously as
he spoke.

" There! don't talk so loud! that old lady
in the white ringlets and the black calash
is looking over her shoulder at you, and
thinks you are an English milord, who has
had too much rum-grog.   They think all
English milords drink ' rum-grog ' by buckets
full, these parleyvooing people."

" Besides," Philip resumed in a sulky but
lower tone, " I have a motive!"

" A motive—excellent! Here we are! Three
cheers for the motive! Everybody for his
motive and Somebody for us all.   Now, let
us have a cigar!"

They stopped on the threshold of one of

those magnificent cigar shops — those temples
devoted to the worship of the smoky god,
whoever he may be, which only Paris possesses.   I say this, without the slightest wish
to depreciate the stately establishments of
Messrs Rees, Milo, Buckingham, Hudson, or
the "African" in Regent Street.   But what
I have said is the fact, and I cannot gainsay
it.

They were about to enter, had the door
half open, when Doctor Ionides turned, and
pointing to a seated figure who was leaning
across the counter, condescendingly chatting
with one of the cigar-serving young ladies,
said to Philip, but in a whisper—

"Look there!"

Philip looked as he was bidden, and saw
the whiskers, the moustache, the grand costume, and the aristocratic mien of Lord Viscount Baddington.

His fingers would have been at his throat
a moment afterwards; but the dexterous
Doctor had him in his iron gripe in an
instant, and hauled him out with such dex-

terity that the young lady and the young
Lord had scarcely time to look up at the
sound of the closing door, when Philip and
the Doctor were safe outside the shop.

" Not now! not now! you fool," the latter
hastily muttered. " Do you want to ruin
all? Do you want to spoil the game? Is
it this dog of a Lord alone that you want to
see? Is there nobody else? I tell you that
we *must* wait till to-night. Then we shall
by able to bag both birds—the hen pheasant
as well as this strutting cock."

" As you will. You are my master for
a time; but beware, I have a will of my own,
and it will assert itself. But I am determined to see him, to confront him, to meet
his eye. I will give you my solemn word of
honour not to molest him, not even to insult
him, till you fix the time and give me the
word."

CHAP. XXXVII.

A HAPPY MARRIAGE.

"SOLEMN word and honour! Solemn
word and fiddlestick! Solemn word
and walnut pickles!" the unceremonious
Doctor Ionides retorted; "but stay, I think
you do really believe in such things; so we
will go in and have a quiet cigar. You'll find
it rather a difficult matter to get one in Paris,
though, my friend."

And so into the gay cigar-shop, where they
purchased their ambiguous weed—the higher-
priced French cigars are, the worse they
usually turn out to be — and added their con-
tribution to the Augean strewings of half-
burnt cigar-lights on the floor. One of the

fair *dames de comptoir* gazed with some curiosity at Doctor Ionides and his notable costume, and simperingly muttered something about being *en carnaval*. The Doctor had always been a gallant man, and he took off his hat, and made the young lady a low bow; whereat she smiled again, and whispered something to Eulalie, her companion, in French.

" *C'est un milord*"—" It is an English nobleman," she might have whispered.

" *Plutôt un mouchard, il porte perruque*"— " A police-agent rather; he wears a wig" — it is not quite improbable that Mademoiselle Eulalie may have doubtingly answered.

" *Un voleur, peut-être*"—" A thief, perhaps" — was another flattering supposition.

" *Ça se peut,*" maybe another.

" *Qu'il est drôle !*" — " How funny."

" *Tiens,*" for which idiomatic expression I should be very much obliged for a literal translation myself.

The whispered colloquy was here put an end to by the entrance of a superb English footman

who wanted " *Doo soo de taback à prisy,
snuffy*, you know, *byang fort; comprenny voo?*"

I wonder which, if any, of the young ladies'
suppositions, with respect to my friend Doctor
Ionides, was the correct one.

Lord Baddington was not alone.   The
episcopal guardsman, indeed, had been de-
tained in England by a grudging country and
an invidious commander-in-chief, to do duty
at some common-place barracks, near Port-
man Square, London; but, *en revanche* (I do
not know how it is, but whenever I find myself
on French ground, in fact or in fiction, I can't
help indulging in a Lilliputian French
quotation now and then), the fiery-faced
major had accompanied his noble friend to
Paris as social aide-de-camp; and the services
of another henchman — for a lord cannot get
on without two toadies — had been secured,
in the person of one Mr. Creamingpett, an
honourable, and a paid *attaché* of the English
Embassy, and who was — what paid *attachés*
of Embassy are, the whole world over.   For
diplomatists are stamped in a limited mint, the

coinage of which, notwithstanding, is wonderfully homogeneous. There is your great ambassadorial crown-piece, gouty, dinner-giving, and occasionally with his *confrères* squabbling. There is the half-crown, or secretary of legation — sharp, thin, *coryphée* pursuing, and against Guatemalean *chargé d'affaires*, or Fee-jee minister plenipotentiary intriguing. There are the pert, shining, glossy, sparkling shilling-and-sixpenny *attachés*, paid and unpaid, waltzing, flirting, late-supping, and occasionally levanting. These coins are passed from hand to hand, or from court to court, just as is the current money of the realm; but there is no difference in ambassadorial coinage between Vienna and Petersburg; and the money-changers of Constantinople will tell you the exact *agio* upon the diplomatic ducats of Stockholm.

Is it not time, though, that you, whose patience, oh, my reader, rivals that of Grissel, famous in mediæval Chaucerian story — exceeds that of him, that literary scoundrel of fair Italia's clime during the middle ages, who having the alternative given to him either to read Guicciardini through or go to the galleys, chose the former, but, breaking down at the ninety-ninth siege of Bologna, went back to the oar and the chain and the cudgel rejoicing — but to that dreadful book no more? Is it not time, long-suffering and forbearing reader of mine, that thou shouldst know why Lord Baddington should be found in a cigar-shop in a Parisian *passage*, with a major and a paid *attaché* for his squires; and why he, they — Philip Leslie, Doctor Ionides — should be, this present night of Mardi Gras, in Paris at all?

Briefly thus:—It will be remembered that Lady Baddington had extorted from her grandnephew a solemn promise that he would not, for the future, at any time molest or interfere with that little " black-eyed dancing-girl, whose name was Manuelita." The promise was made in the golden Autumn time, when the woods wore their richest dresses, and there was great joy among trees bearing rich fruit. Pleased with the promptness of her relative to promise, her Ladyship had evinced her gratitude by generously presenting him with a cheque for a thousand pounds, adding, that if he behaved himself, there was no knowing where her liberality, financially speaking, might stop; for that she intended to marry a duke, and to have, not a miserable jointure of twenty thousand pounds, but thirty thousand, at least, *per annum.* Lord Baddington told the anecdote cheerfully at his clubs, amidst great applause. Various comments, but all of them favourable, were made on his beautiful grand-aunt, and unanimous verdict being passed that she was a " splendid woman," and bets were laid as to the particular duke who would, eventually, have the honour of leading her to the hymeneal altar. That he was an aged duke seemed settled, too, by general consent, Major Gambroon facetiously remarking, "that such a beauty was the old peer's best companion."

Now, the ostensible motive for the Lady Baddington's making her grand-nephew so promise was this: that she had made up her imperial mind that Manuelita was to marry Philip Leslie, and that the two were to be very fond of one another, and were to be happy together all "the days of their lives. There was no disparity of age — no disparity of station—a painter and a dancing-girl—*cela se comprend*. No disparity of temper, for they were both spoiled children; and both, her Ladyship deigned to observe, very good-looking children too. Her Ladyship was in the right. A handsomer pair had hardly been seen since John Lord Hervey married Molly Lepell.

So they were to be married, and all the rest of it. It was astonishing what a hurry the Lady Baddington was in to see them married — how she chafed and fretted — nay, almost how cross she became at the delay. They were to be married, and to be happy. She had obtained numerous commissions for Philip already. He was to paint large pictures, be a Royal Academician, make his fortune, be knighted, *que sais-je?* — only they were to be married immediately.

Was Philip very much in love with Manuelita, I wonder? He was in love with himself, with the goodness and beauty of his patroness, with his new-born fortune, with a fine studio, and brave canvases and lay figures, and plenty of ultramarine and megilp. He was in love with clothes and regular victuals, and exemption from the tyranny of a lodging-house-keeper. Yes; and I think he must have been in love, too, with the dark eyes and pouting lips, and artless ways of his future wife; but, such was his sense of gratitude to his benefactress, that I am persuaded, had she brought him by the hand, or rather paw, to that poor baboon-woman, whose picture on the walls has lately been disgusting the town, and whose public exhibition was an insult to public decency and an insult to our system of police, and said to him, "Philip Leslie! behold your bride; you must love her very much, and be happy together for the rest of your lives," Philip would have bowed the knee, and hied at once to Doctors' Commons, for his name to be filled up on the orthodox

parchment containing the benediction of his
Grace the Archbishop of Canterbury and a
blue stamp, in conjunction with the bearded
lady. Men go very cheap; brag of devotion,
honour, disinterestedness, and so on, as we
may, we sell ourselves, now to pay off some
debts, and now to increase some luxuries;
now for a new steam-engine for the " works,"
now for a new cab-horse. And even your
very disinterested lovers make " time-bar-
gains " at the altar, as they would in Capel
Court. They buy for the account, and specu-
late for a rise; but, ah me! what a dreadful
wailing and gnashing of teeth there is when a
nipping "fall" comes among the bulls and the
bears.

Thus, as the Lady Baddington had said, *sic
volo sic jubeo*, Philip had no course to pursue,
but to acquiesce in the decision of that
amiable match-maker. Don't you know, then,
those dear, delightful, indefatigable assassin-
esses, who are charmingly determined to "find
a wife" for every lonely bachelor they come
across, and pursue him with daggers dressed

in myrtle, like Harmodius, and poisoned chalices wreathed in flowers — marrying him to
smiling shrews, affable dragons, mild-eyed
scorpions, and Syren-voiced sea-serpents;
Venus Aphrodites, who scratch your face,
and Clios who confiscate your latch-key, lock
up your tobacco-jar, and tell you, with the
supremest unconcern in the world, that they
have thrown your pet cutty-pipe, which took
you months to colour, into the dust-hole, as a
"nasty, dirty thing." I knew such a match-
maker once (Heaven rest her bones! for she is
with the saints), who wanted to marry me to
a woman who had a wart on the left side of
her nose, and a pair of shoulders that you
might have hung a week's washing upon, so
horizontal were they. She thought she had
me hard and fast; but I saved myself by
flight to the Channel Islands, for I am certain
that woman (Warty) would have had my life
(with sheer kindness) within six months after
marriage. Her name was not HELEN, alas!
And who is Helen, now, I should like to
know? Bah! I sit at the *Porte Scie*, and

adore Helen as she goes by, and forgive her, for her beauty's sake, all the woes she has caused to Troy; *mais, quant à son amour, je ne m'en soucie plus guère: et d'autres* — Helen jilted me, and I am consoled.

The wedding was postponed, unavoidably, to the commencement of the new year, Eighteen hundred and thirty-six, in consequence of a very serious fit of illness which befell her Ladyship of Baddington; and during one crisis of which, her very life was despaired of. She was attended throughout by her body surgeon, Sir Paracelsus Fleem, in consultation with whom was the great Sir Samuel Skryer, he who wrote that wondrous book on abnormal neuralgia of zymotic pimples, and was own physician to Queen Adelaide; and the apothecary employed (truly assiduous was he in his attendance) was one Mr. Tinctop, of Drury Lane. Her Ladyship recovered, to look more beautiful than ever; and every preparation having been made for the auspicious event, it was finally arranged to take place on the Fourth of February.

Everybody was very happy; the beauteous convalescent especially. Manuelita was happier than anybody, of course. It is quite consonant with young ladies who are about to be married to cry a good deal, and sit a good deal alone in corners, thinking, doubtless, of the greater bliss in store for them. Manuelita took the fullest advantage of both those privileges; so much so, that Lady Baddington rated her occasionally, and asked her whether she were moping. She could not have been moping, you know. Her patroness was very good to her. She was installed in the fairy palace in Curzon Street, where her affianced husband paid her visits at certain times and under strict surveillance. The footmen were commanded to do her reverence, the ladies' maids (Lady Baddington had two) to pay her as much attention as though she were their mistress. Even the hall porter unbent to her, and called her "Miss." Mr. Tinctop, the apothecary from Drury Lane—(and "owever my lady can habide sich low karackters, and from sich neighbourhoods, Hi can't hunderstand" (*sic* cook in *cog. loq.*) —- Mr. Tinctop, who was a good deal about the house, took much notice of little Manuelita.

The Viscountess, who was indefatigable in the matter, had written to the dear child's uncle at Liverpool, discreetly, or at least ingeniously, accounting for her absence, vouching for her good conduct, and informing him of his niece's approaching union with a young man " moving (O platitude of platitudes!) in a respectable sphere of life." The equally respectable but irascible Señor contented himself by sending up his Curse by return of post, recommending his niece, with much urgency, to the especial care of the Principle of Evil. He added, in a postcript, that the absence of Manuelita had been to him a pecuniary loss of one hundred pounds sterling; and that he would be exceedingly obliged if the English lady, who was aiding and abetting her in her undutiful practices, would remit him that sum per bank post-bill.

Lady Baddington laughed, and put the letter in the fire.

There was a night of anxious suspense, and
pleasurable anticipation — it is to be hoped to
all parties concerned — but certainly to this
matrimonial Lady Bountiful who wore the
Baddington coronet. She had provided the
bride's trousseau; she had chosen the wedding
dress, fixed upon its colour, determined its
pattern, devised its trimmings; she, with her
own hands, tried it on the shrinking form of
the blushing little bride expectant, by the
light of her own pink wax toilette-table
candles; she threw over her shoulders a rich
shot silk mantle; she adjusted on the nestling
head a wondrous structure of inscrutable millinery called a bonnet; — for it was winter,
and she was to be married in a bonnet; she
imprinted a loving kiss on the girl's lips; and
expatiated on the happiness she would experience in the life-long companionship of so
clever, generous, good-hearted a husband.
Then she opened a morocco case, like a crimson oyster-shell, and showed Manuelita a glittering toy of emeralds and brilliants, which
she intended to be her special wedding pre-

sent. The marriage was to take place, not at St. George's or any such ostentatious edifice, but at a quiet old church in the city, where there was a rector who was very old and very deaf, a very low Churchman, and who cured the souls of his parishioners, ten months out of the twelve, at a briny little watering-place on the Sussex coast; and where the curate (who was reported to take, commonly, no human sustenance, save haricot beans and un-buttered muffins) was a furious Tractarian of the most milk-and-water description, and read sermons, which were paraphrases of the "Tracts for the Times" (just then in vogue) every Sunday to a congregation composed of Lady Mumruffin's charity boys, the clerk, the sexton, the sexton's wife, Mr. Deputy Podge's maiden sister, who was supposed not to be quite right in her head, and the carved and gilt lion and unicorn that kept guard at either angle of the churchwardens' pew.

Lord Baddington had not been to his grand-aunt's house for at least two months. His Lordship had sent in his "papers" to the

Horse Guards, and was negotiating the sale of his commission, his extensive estates in Ireland demanding (in the interest of his tenantry, doubtless) all his time and attention. With this view he had crossed St. George's Channel, and was taking care of his estates at Morrison's Hotel, Dublin, where he found the Sneyd's claret not at all unpalatable, and whence he sent frequent and anxiously kind inquiries after Lady Baddington's health.

The marriage-morning came: as the morning, however long deferred, *must* come; the morning for joy, and the morning for sorrow; the morning for you, your Majesty, to be crowned — for you, Jack Suspercoll, to be hanged; the morning for every one of us to lay by crinoline and all-round collars, when the gay pictures shall be turned with their faces to the wall, and those about us open the windows, that our souls may have elbow-room to flee away from the clay.

The bridegroom was dressed, and, pale and palpitating, was waiting in the musty old vestry-room of Saint Duffabox-under-Crump,

Crump Lane, City, for the arrival of his bride, who was to be driven there in Lady Badding- ton's own carriage. Her considerate Ladyship, Philip, being quite a stranger in London, had provided him, even, with a groomsman, in the person of a Mr. Tinctop, apothecary, of Drury Lane, who, in a yellow waistcoat, which gave him in an intense degree the semblance of a canary bird, and a bald head seemingly ex- pressly bees'-waxed and polished for the occasion, so shining was it, moused about the vestry-room, and cunningly contemplated the portrait of the Reverend Doctor Mudgett, rector (resting his hand on a corpulent copy of Hooker's Ecclesiastical Polity), and carefully perused all the placards on the walls relative to baptisms, marriages, churchings, and burial fees.

Time — eleven, sharp.   Clergyman quite ready. Married some blue pilot cloth, brass buttons, and a mahogany-looking hand at- tached to the Trinity House — perhaps an " elder brother," more probably a pilot, to a tremendous bonnet, and a vast circumference of black silk, whose occupant on ordinary days transacted business of a piscatorial nature in Billingsgate Market. Married a messenger of Doctors' Commons, to the mistress of Lady Mumruffin's charity school for girls. Married two or three other people, who evidently did'nt know what they were about, or they would have known better.

Noon: no bride. Twenty minutes, half-past, a quarter to; no bride. Bridegroom almost in frenzy. Mr. Tinctop wiping his bald head, clerk very fidgetty about his fees. Pew-opener ditto. Clergyman impatient, looking at his watch, thinking of his dinner (one bean and a muffin), the people he had to bury in the afternoon, and his unfinished sermon upon St. Simon Stylites, as compared with St. Dominic the Cuirassier.

Ten minutes to, five minutes to; no bride; but AT one, came tearing up to the door one of the high yellow cabs with the big wheels, and the driver sitting on a perch at one side, which were beginning in those days to super-sede the lumbering old hackney coaches.

From this vehicle descended, with as much celerity as his never abandoned dignity would permit, that same resplendent flunkey who had been sent by Lady Baddington with the message about the money the first night that Philip had ever set eyes on her in the Wardour Street curiosity shop.

He wanted Mr. Leslie immediately. Mr. Leslie rushed into the vestibule, knocked against open pew-doors, stumbling over hassocks, and nearly frightening three old pauper women—in incessant quest of the clergyman for port wine, flannel petticoats, and "stuff for the rheumatiz"—nearly out of their lives.

"Jump in," cried the footman; "my lady wants yer d'rectly."

And away they went; the charity boys, who were playing pitch-and-toss close to the niche, where once was the statue of the sainted Duffabox, wondering; and the old applewoman at the corner of Crump Lane lifting up her hands in mute astonishmant. Mr. Tinctop, not very disturbed, as far as his outward seeming went, courteously explained to the clergyman that there must be a screw loose somewhere, though these were not the exact words he used; feed the clerk, the pew-opener and the beadle, who loudly expressed their opinion that he was a "real gentleman," and very carefully folding up the marriage license, which, in consideration of the sum of three pounds twelve shillings and sixpence, his Grace the Archbishop of Canterbury had been kind enough to grant to his well-beloved Philip and Manuelita, placed it in his trousers-pocket, and putting his hands in both those sartorial appendages, placidly wended his way westward.

"If that thing with the blue seal wasn't parchment," he said to himself, alluding, it is to be presumed, to the license, "one could cut it up for curl papers. Stay, it would do capitally to cover a penny-drum with. I don't see what other use we could turn it to. I thought how it would be. I needn't be in a hurry. There's sure to be a blow-up, and I may as well get there when it's all over. Polly's a divine creature, but she has a Temper,

that's undeniable." And it is also a fact, that
Mr. Tinctop hurried himself so little, that
he stopped at the Cathedral Coffee-house in
St. Paul's Churchyard, and comforted himself
with a steaming bowl of mulligatawny soup.
I tell you, using the novelist's prescience, that
which the man *said* to himself; what he really
thought in the innermost tabernacle of his
heart, behind the iconostast of self-deceit, it is
not for me to know—*nec si sciam dicere ausim.*
Few men lie as much, if not more, to themselves, than they lie to others; and in very
many cases, when you *say* to yourself that it
is "all right," you *think*, and are perfectly
convinced that it is "all wrong."

Twenty-five minutes' furious driving brought
the cab, the cabman, the footman, and the
"bridegroom," to the door of Lady Baddington's residence. To the reiterated and pas-
sionate queries of the excited painter, the
footman had but one answer to give—that he
"dursn't tell for his life—that his lady had
bidden him not to." Just, however, as they
neared the doors—and just after, it may be,

that something bright and yellow had rested
for a moment in his palm, before it was con-
signed to the pocket of his crimson plush
waistcoat—he whispered, so affrightedly that
some of the powder from his ambrosial curls
was sprinkled on Philip's coat-collar, these
remarkable words—

"SHE'S BOLTED!"

"Who has bolted?"

"And there's a devil of a row!"

This was certainly not an answer to the
point; but there was no time to give another;
for the cab stopped, the house door opened,
and the footman disappeared among the other
flunketry.

Up-stairs in the drawing-room the painter
found Lady Baddington alone, raging in her
weeds—a beautiful black jaguar. She rushed
at him, rather than to meet him; and when he
stooped to make his customary obeisance—for
she liked to be treated as a queen always—
flung him on one side with a swirl of her
drapery.

"What have you done with your wife, you

fool?" she began in her passion; but she relented, and continued in kind accents, though her voice quivered with the rage that was within her,—"My poor Philip, I know that it is not your fault; but you have lost your wife."

"Heavens and earth, Madam! Can it be true that—"

"She has fled this house. She is gone away. How she went I don't know; but the time must have been between nine and ten this morning. I was dressing in my own room. I had ordered Mickwith (lady's maid number two) to dress her; but she begged and prayed to be left to herself for half-an-hour, and alone she was left. The hall porter was away from his post. I discharged him on the spot. She must have slid down stairs, the little lizard, and so out of the house."

She sat down in a great *fauteuil*, panting with suppressed anger. Then resumed—

"She had put on her plainest, meanest dress. Every gown, every trinket, every ornament I had given her, were there, strewn about the room. On the dressing table was this letter. Read it."

She sent a half-sheet of note paper fluttering towards Philips, and emptying a flask of *eau-de-Cologne* on her handkerchief, buried her face in the cambric; but not to weep.

It was a hurried, timorous scrawl, and ran thus—

"*I cannot help it. I know how wicked, ungrateful, undeserving I am ; but I love him. Pray dear Philip to forgive me. Pray to him to forget me. I shall never come back. Don't seek for me. Oh! my lady, if you knew how miserable I am, you would forgive me too.*

"MANUELITA."

And no more, save that the paper was blotted all over with scarcely yet dried tears.

"What do you intend?" the Lady asked abruptly.

The poor fellow never had much presence of mind; and now it was five thousand miles distant. He stammered out—

" Seek her."

" Seek her! Where?"

Philip was silent.

"Do you know with WHOM she is gone away?" Lady Baddington asked, slowly and deliberately. "She has fled—bah! she has run away with my accomplished grandnephew, with that fair-faced devil from the pit, the unutterable villain, Lord Baddington."

"Good heavens!"

"I tell you that with that man, and with none other, she has run away to shame, to dishonour, to disgrace! *Where* she is, I'll find out within four-and-twenty hours. As for the girl, if I had her here, I'd have her whipped to death with knotted cords. As for that titled hound, he has broken his promise, and he shall die, by——"

She stayed the utterance of a fearful oath, and placed her pretty hand on her mouth, then with a bitter smile:

"You did'nt think I could swear, Philip; but I can, and I can do what I swear to."

It is not exactly my purpose how Lady Baddington contrived to obtain the information she desired. That she did obtain it is certain; and it was in consequence of the information just mentioned, that Philip Leslie was in Paris; that he was accompanied by Dr. Ionides, that both had procured tickets for the great *Bal Masqué* at the Opera, which takes place on the night of Mardi Gras.

CHAP. XXXVIII.

BEFORE THE BALL.

IN an upper chamber *maison garnie*, of that special street of furnished apartments, that Percy Street relique of Paris, the Rue Louis-le-Grand, and about eleven at night on Mardi Gras, Philip Leslie and Doctor Ionides were dressing for the ball. It should with more rigid propriety be explained, that the Doctor had completed the preliminaries of his toilet in one apartment, while his friend had arrayed himself for the *festin* in another; but their two bed-chambers were immediately contiguous, opened one upon the other, in fact; and the Doctor had left the inner room and entered that of Philip, in order that the latter might have an opportunity of criticising the splendour of his array previous to his putting the finishing touches thereto.

Mr. Philip Leslie had never been at a masquerade in his life; and with settled obstinacy this singular young man pertinaciously refused to travesty himself in any way, even to the assuming of a domino, and persisted in dressing himself in a plain suit of evening black, which a regard for truth compels me to say became him remarkably well. With scorn he had contemplated the whole stock-in-trade of M. Raphael-ben-Daoud, costumier and *marchant fripier* of the Temple and the Rue de Seine, and had turned a deaf ear to the serpent who had striven to enchant him with the sight of gay and resplendent costumes—troubadours, pages, Louis Quinze marquises, Louis Treize cavaliers, men-at-arms, arquebusiers, and the like. He was not going to make a fool of himself, he said; so adhered to his evening suit of black—although I should be glad, by the way, to know if in the whole annal's of Folly's wardrobe there has even been made mention of a suit of attire more preposterously foolish than that same "evening dress" with which we *affoible* ourselves ' when we go out to dinner, or to the Honourable Mrs. Blank's Thursdays. Thanking heaven as I am glad to do sincerely for most things—meat, drink, decent raiment, good books, and the companionship of dear friends—there is yet one thing for which I am even more devoutly grateful: that it is not often my lot to be asked out to polite dinner parties, and that my mantel-piece is seldom cumbered with the Honourable Mrs. Blank's cards. *Timeo Danaos:* I fear that dreadful dress-coat of the evening, that sable anomaly, that long-tailed excrescence, half-bird, half-buffoon like, and which always makes me think of Vinny Bournes' lines on the jackdaw:—

> " There is a bird, who by his coat,
> And by the hoarseness of his note,
> You might proclaim a crow."

My good friend, Mr. Lumley of her Majesty's Theatre, is good enough at the commencement of every season, to place my name on

the free-list of his establishment; yet I declare, that during the summer last past I
missed seeing Piccolomini no less than eleven
times, owing to my horror for the tail-coat.
Yet it is astonishing what importance is
attached to this ludicrous, unseemly, unmean-
ing garment. They won't let you look at the
pictures in the Hermitage at St. Petersburg
unless you have a tail-coat on; you must
even pay your morning visits in the vile
thing; and a Russian Countess, to whom I
once had a letter of introduction, positively
cut me after the first interview, because I
called on her in a cut-away coat. It was
from a Petropolitan tailor, too, and had cost
me forty roubles, cash. " *Il est venu me voir
en froc: un épicier : quoi?*" she said.

The views of Doctor Ionides, with respect
to the proper costume to be worn at a *bal
masqué*, were of a nature totally opposed to
those entertained by his friend. The Doctor
had a pictorial taste and picturesque imagination, and delighted in gay and rich apparel.
He had revolved in his mind the relative

expediency of an almost infinite variety of fancy dresses, including those of a male *débardeur,* a *fort de la halle,* and a *pierrot,* and had at last fixed upon an astounding equipment, certainly appertaining to no particular age or country, but which partook of the characteristics of all. It consisted of a cuirass formed of gilt scales, a scarlet mantle, a plaid skirt, fleshings, top-boots, a Roman helmet and a tremendously long Spanish rapier. The Doctor had preserved the use of his green spectacles; and, after much anxious deliberation and nice weighing of the proprieties of the thing, he had determined on affixing to his already sufficiently developed nasal organ, an enormous false nose in pasteboard, coloured in the most violent red. This, as the novelists, who delight in describing the wardrobes of the last century, say, "completed his costume;" and he was in the act of fixing on the rubicund appendage I have alluded to, at this same time of eleven of the clock.

"A touch of rouge on either cheek," the Doctor remarked, complacently, "and I am entirely at your service. Am I going to wear white kid gloves? Certainly not. I see that you are about to assume those luxuries; but I repudiate them : in the first place, because I consider them to be vanities, mockeries, delusions and snares; secondly, because lemon-coloured kids are more fashionable; thirdly, because no human glover ever made a pair of kids sufficiently large to fit these hands of mine."

He held out, as he spoke, a gigantic pair of hands, the fingers in their gnarled thickness and clumsiness strongly resembling the great crimson wooden monstrosities that hang over glovers' shops. They were not very unlike them in colour, either.

Both were now ready for departure; and Doctor Ionides was suggesting the expediency of blowing out the candles, and telling the *concièrge* to fetch a vehicle to convey them to the opera-house in the Rue Lepelletier, when Philip stopped him.

" Before we start on this expedition, POLLY-BLANK," he commenced—

" Ionides, Ionides, my dear friend," interrupted the other, holding up one of the large
hands with a gesture of caution; " Doctor
Ionides, if you please. Pollyblank, if that
mythical personage ever existed, is dead and
buried. Transported beyond the seas for the
term of his natural life. Confined in one of
the secret dungeons of the Spielberg. He
languishes beneath the *piombi* of the ducal
palace of Venice. He is at Cayenne, at Nouka-
kioa. He is in a chain-gang at Perth, Swan-
River, Western Australia. He went up in a
balloon, and has never since been heard of.
Pollyblank was blown to pieces in the Gun-
powder Plot; and Ionides rose, Phœnix-like,
from his ashes. Pray be cautious, imprudent
youth. Even French lodging-house walls may
have ears, and little birds may be waiting
round the corners to carry the name of Pollyblank to his Majesty's justices of the peace,
the judges of his Majesty's Central Criminal
Court, and the governors of his Majesty's
jail."

" Well, then, Ionides—Doctor Ionides, if
you like."

" I am all attention."

" Tell me, then, what is to be our definite and settled purpose to-night?"

" Have you come all these miles without knowing it?" the Doctor somewhat disdainfully asked. " What a man of wind and water you are, to be sure. Didn't our gracious lady give you ample instructions? Doesn't your own sense of wrong and outrage tell you plainly what course you ought to adopt? Is there any purpose on earth for which you ought to have come here but to kill Lord Baddington?"

" I don't like killing a man in cold blood," was Philip's reply. He had thrown himself on a sofa, and was moving himself restlessly about. " It seems dastardly, mean, cruel. If you had allowed me to speak to him in that cigar-shop, where he sat, with his toad-eaters, grinning at me like a baboon, I would have told him that he was a ruffian, and knocked him down then and there. If he had chosen to challenge and fight me afterwards, well and good. But I can't bear the thought of going to a masquerade for the express purpose of quarrelling with a man, however great a scoundrel he may be, and fighting a duel with him. It's taking a low, cowardly advantage."

" Not so great an advantage," the Doctor complacently retorted. " Can you fence ?"

" Very little."

" Supposing that he, being the insulted party, and having the right to the choice of weapons, weere to choose swords ? They fight a good deal with swords in France."

" Well !"

" Suppose that he, being a cavalry officer a blustering, swaggering, dragoon—were to know how to use his sabre to *his* advantage?"

" What then ?"

" Supposing — to put an end to supposition —that he were to kill you instead of your killing him ? "

" I should be out of a world I am sick of."

" Misanthropy granted — and I don't believe in yours, by the way; for I am satisfied that there is nothing you would like better than to live to be fifty years of age, and to have five thousand a-year — the advantage is neither on one side nor the other. As regards my not permitting you to have a collision with the fellow in the cigar shop, I had my reasons for that. I am acting, I have acted all along, under instructions. If it hadn't been for me, you would never have known where to find the man who has robbed you of your sweetheart, and who, by the living jingo, has seduced her."

" It's a lie," cried Philip, starting up from the sofa, with a fierce cry of rage. " Villain as he is, he has never dared to wrong her. She resisted him before. She has resisted him now, successfully."

" I tell you," Doctor Ionides repeated, with bitter emphasis, " that he *has* seduced her; that she is his mistress; that he is living with her now in a snug little *entresol* in the Rue Taitbout. They go to the theatre together, they drive into the Bois de Boulogne together; they will be at the masquerade together, this very night.

" I say again that it is false."

" Bah ! we are men. Don't let 's have any more child's talk about it. Now look you here, Philip Leslie. You know me well enough by this time. Known me as conjurer, mountebank, adventurer, convict, forger, scoundrel, anything you like. But I am a bigger man than you, simply because I have a WILL. You boasted of yours just now, Philip! What is it?—A curd of pigeon's milk, a cobweb net, a rope of sand ! If that will had been properly directed twenty years ago, it might have made me a very different man. It might have made me honest, industrious, prosperous; it might have made me a happy man at home, with children round my knees. But it is too late to talk of all that now. Jack Pollyblank's will, that he brags so much about, has only served to guide him through dark and crooked ways, and he is alone now —desolate, lost; with no one but the devil to help him, for Heaven will not."

He uttered these last words in accents very different from the boastful, defiant swagger of diction in which he ordinarily indulged. He paused, and was for some moments silent, standing there a strange sight in his absurd and uncouth dress, his huge beard and green spectacles. Who would believe me if I were to say, that the spectacles were, if only for a moment, dimmed with an unaccustomed moisture; and that two drops of brine rolled down the painted cheeks of Jack Pollyblank?

Scoundrels are human. Thieves are not always thieving; they think sometimes of their childhood — of the time before they thieved. The man who murdered the Italian boy, set him to play with his children before he slew him.

"I have wandered from the subject," Doctor Ionides resumed, in an altered voice; "and, unless I am very much mistaken, the hand of the clock points to twenty to twelve. We must be at the ' crib ' by midnight. All the fun of the fair begins at midnight. Before we go, I have one little thing to ask you. Are you very much in love with Manuelita?"

"How can you ask me?" the Painter cried, indignantly.

" Because I firmly believe that you don't care twopence-halfpenny about her. You are angry with this sprig of nobility for making you ridiculous, and would like to shoot him, if you had a chance; but as regards the girl, I think you are of the opinion of the gentleman who dismounted from the mare that was a kicker, and that you think you are 'well out of it.' Isn't that so?"

" I shall not answer your question," Philip replied moodily. "You seem to be my Mephistophiles, and to surround me with your infernal spells and enchantments. Now that the girl has jilted me, that fop of a Lord, you, or anybody,—down to the shoeblack on the Boulevard yonder — may have her for me. But I did love her very dearly."

" You did nothing of the sort," was the pertinacious denial of the Doctor. " If you had valued her at two straws, you would not have suffered me, whose former and peculiar acquaintance with little Manuelita you remember, to have anything to do with the matter. Philip Leslie, I will tell you with

whom you have all along been in love, and
with whom you are in love now."

The blood mantled up to Philip's forehead
when he heard these words. He began to
stammer out an indignant denial; but checked
himself, and said simply—

"And with whom am I in love, pray, since
you know my affairs so well?"

"With the mistress of us all — Génévieve,
Viscountess Baddington."

"You are exceedingly insolent, Mr. Poll —
Doctor Ionides."

"I always was troubled with that com-
plaint," rejoined the Doctor coolly. "I slept
next to an impudent boy at school, and perhaps I caught it from him. It's no good
your telling me that you're not in love with
the bewitching Viscountess. I am. I am of
a loving disposition. Didn't I make love to
Manuelita, once upon a time? We all are.
Now, without pressing you too hard, for I see
you're chafing like a horse under a hard bit,
wouldn't you do anything in the world to
please the lady who has been your benefactress, and is your friend?"

" Anything — everything ! " Philip cried, enthusiastically.

" Wouldn't you obey her slightest commands ? "

" I would ! "

" Well, then, not her slight, but her serious commands are, that you obey me in every particular. Will this satisfy you ? "

He handed Philip a tiny slip of rose-coloured paper in a scented envelope. The contents were in Lady Baddington's beautiful Italian hand — Philip knew it well; for her Ladyship had, on more than one occasion, condescended to write to him. In this billet she intimated her wish, that he should follow implicitly the directions given him by the person who accompanied him to Paris. And it was signed, G.—G for Géneviève, it is to be presumed; for her Ladyship had, when she so chose, none of the ordinary haughtiness of rank, and was fond of calling herself by her own pretty Christian name.

Philip returned the missive — he could not doubt its authenticity—with a deep sigh; and

Doctor Ionides, once more becoming the humorous philosopher, whose guise he generally affected, surveyed himself with great complacency in a cheval glass, and then, humming a cheerful tune, intimated his opinion that it was pretty nearly time to be moving.

The pair cast long cloaks over their shoulders — long cloaks were worn in 1836 — and descending the stairs, were soon ensconsed in a *fiacre*, and on their way to the Grand Opera.

CHAP. XXXIX.

THE BALL.

PARIS had made up its mind to be exceedingly gay all night long. Very seldom, indeed, does fair Lutetia so "keep it up;" and with all the gaiety and dissipation of that which is said to be the liveliest capital in Europe, there is, on ordinary occasions, very little stirring that is worth seeing in Paris after midnight. But a *bal masqué* at the Grand Opera is an occasion on which the Parisians forget their generally-early habits, and when the disturbance of the peaceful slumbers of *concierges* is disregarded in a city, in which, as a rule, there are no latch-keys. *Mardi-gras* stands on the threshold of the

grim *carême*—the forty days of Lent, with its
fastings and its penances; and in a country in
whose religion there is a large admixture of
enthusiasm (albeit France is by no means the
most Catholic of Catholic lands), the unre-
served and almost frantic merriment of a
saturnalia immediately preceding a season of
abstinence and tribulation can be readily understood and accounted for.

Do not think that the grand opera masquerade is the only one that takes place in
Paris on the night of Shrove Tuesday. Such
entertainments pullulate all over the capital.
There are masked balls at all the great dancing
saloons: the Prado, the Salles Valentino and
Sainte Cécile, the "Wauxhall," and the Salle
Barthélemy. There are balls at the barriers;
there are balls at several of the minor theatres.
At the period of which I write, there were
reckoned among the sights—and by some
among the scandals too—of Paris, that famous
"*Descente de la · Courtille*," now degenerated
into a mean jostling of haggard disreputables
clad in faded frippery; but which twenty years

ago was a very grand, gay, amusing, wicked
scene indeed; a sort of smudged sketch from
Nicholas Poussin—all Fauns and Bacchantes,
Silenuses and Satyrs over-brimming chalices
and roaring songs, vine-leaves, leopard-skins,
pipes and tobacco, rouge, spangles, flambeaux,
and finery. Paris knows such out-door orgies
no longer. The inebriate jollities of the *courtille* can only be enacted now *à huis clos*, in
the sanctuary of some *cabinet particulier* of
the *Maison Dorée*, or in some *petite maison*
of the Bois de Boulogne, where Russian princes
and magnates of the Bourse may amuse themselves in counterfeiting the amusements of the
lowest classes of the population. It is edifying
how outwardly staid and externally decorous
my Paris is becoming. It gambles still, but
in the Five per Cents *Rentes;* it speculates
not on the chances of the *Tapis Vert*, but in
the investments of the *Grand Livre.* It sings,
but no longer at the *Caveau,* or *Enfants de
Silène;* it is morally naughty still, but its
dames aux camellias die penitent and phthisical;
its *filles de marbre* deliver moral apophthegms;

and its *dames aux perles* read Thomas à
Kempis. No wicked pictures in Parisian
shops or on Parisian *quais* now; no *galeries
de bois* in the Palais Royal; no Frascati's, no
Bonjean's. Even the shops begin to be closed
on Sundays; going to church is becoming
fashionable; and auricular confession is reckoned rather *bon ton* than otherwise. It
would seem as though that strange, stern,
inexplicable man who holds France in his iron
grasp—who sits aloft and aloof, an imperial
owl, boding, mysterious, carnivorous, immove-
able, wise, and blind to the broad noon-day
glare of public opinion and the aspirations of
millions of men for rational freedom, yet far-
seeing in the black night of tumult and trouble,
has resolved in a sort of cynical remorse for
his own early excesses to make Paris moral in
spite of itself. Yes, he who has gone through
the whole curriculum of the *viveur's* wild
existence ; who has diced and drunk and
heard the chimes at midnight, and long after
midnight, with Stanley and Chesterfield,
d'Orsay and Brunswick, whose name was on

every discounter's bill, and against whom
every discounter had his writ, has sternly determined to put down at least the outward
semblance of immorality in an abandoned
capital. It is not the devil sick and wishing
a monk to be; but the devil putting on a
shovel hat and a white tie, tucking his tail
beneath the folds of his silk apron, and setting
his attendant imps to chant Sternhold and
Hopkins instead of skylarking with red-hot
pitchforks. Stranger things may happen, do
happen every day, and yet may not be incon-
sistent. Yet may the world see Cæsars, owing
two millions of money, bringing bills into the
Senate for the punishment of fraudulent bank-
rupts; Syllas speechifying before the Plebs
against capital punishment, and denouncing
the intolerable atrocity of casting malefactors
from the Tarpeian rock; Mirabeaus moving
that the infraction of the seventh command-
ment should be made felony; and Justice
Fieldings sending Bacchanalians to Bridewell
for riotous conduct at the Rose, or Tom King's
Coffee-house.

Philip, who was naturally nervous, did not experience much inward satisfaction at the companionship, in a hackney carriage, of an individual attired in the, to say the least,' conspicuous style of Doctor Ionides, and was not at all certain as to the reception which his grotesquely-accoutred friend would meet with from the multitude which would probably be assembled at the door of the opera-house; but in this he only showed his inexperience and want of knowledge of Parisian life; for had he chosen to go dressed as a Cherokee Indian —wore paint, tomahawk, feathered mocassins, trophies of gore, bedewed with scalp and all— and had the Doctor assumed the semblance of an ostrich, or an elephant, or the colossus of Rhodes, or the tower of Babel, the crowd would have taken the travesties in good part, and saluted them as right worthy keepers up of the carnival.

"I remember," the Doctor remarked, as they rattled along the Boulevard, "going to this same grand opera turn-out two years ago, dressed as Robert the Devil—no, I mean the

other fellow—the man with the striped legs,
the beard, and the bass voice—Bertram.
There was a gentleman there too, dressed as
the postillion of Longjumeau.   Tremendous
jack-boots he had, and all Coventry in ribbons
on his hat.   We fell out about an undersized
party with corkscrew ringlets and black velvet
trousers, who was a *débardeur* there, but a milliner's assistant when she was at home.   The
postillion was very good at the *savate*, and very
nearly succeeded in catching me an ugly blow
under the chin with the left toe of the jack-
boots.   Then I knocked him down.   Then,
while he sat crying on the ground (they always
cry when they are hit), a gendarme caught
me round the waist, and I knocked him down
too.   Then, I think, they must have called in
the artillery too, and the fire-brigade, and the
sappers and miners; at all events, I was cap-
tured by a whole army, and conducted to the
nearest *poste*—the *violon* they call it—that's a
station-house in England.   They took the
postillion too—I suppose because he had been
knocked down, and had so brought discredit

upon *La Belle France*, or perhaps because his
jack-boots were too much like those of the
gendarmerie, and were considered libellous.
At the *poste* they made the same polite inquiries as to my age, my birthplace, and my
papa and mamma, without asking which they
don't seem to be able to manage anything in
France. Then all the officials on duty shook
their heads very gravely, as if to imply that I
must expect to be sent to the galleys at the
very least for knocking a man down; and
then they locked me and the postilion up in
the *violon*. There were two or three more
jolly post-boys there, and one or two *forts de
la halle*, with a sprinkling of *chiffoniers* (rag-
pickers), drunken *blouses*, beggars, and thieves.
Everybody was as drunk as he could wish to
be, and we were merry indeed. First we sang
the 'Marseillaise,' and then we danced the
'Cancan,' and then we all fell to kicking violently at the door. They very soon opened it
in answer to our summons; but what do you
think it was to do? So sure as my name is—
well, never mind what it is; you know well

enough—the atrocious myrmidons of a hideous despotism made an irruption into the cell, and there and then, without asking who was in fault, stripped every living soul in that miserable dungeon of their boots or shoes. It was no use resisting. Tyranny was triumphant. But you should have seen, or rather heard the row in the morning, when, previous to taking us up before the Commissary of Police, they let us out into a court-yard, and bade us, every one of us, *réclamer* or claim our own property again. There were the boots and shoes all of a heap—all higgledy-piggledy. Such a scene I never witnessed before or after. Of course everybody wanted the best pair of upper leathers he could lay his foot to. For my own part, I think I came away with one patent-leather slipper and one of my friend the postillion's jack-boots."

"And how did it end? Were you fined or imprisoned, or both?"

"Neither. In his unshod condition, the postillion became mollified; and I believe that about four o'clock in the morning we swore eternal friendship. When taken before the Commissary in the morning, the original gendarme was not forthcoming. There was, to be sure, a supplementary one, who swore that I was dressed as Robert Macaire, and that I danced prohibited dances; but his evidence went for nothing. In fact, there seemed to be a general confusion of ideas as to who was whom—or had been whom, the night before; and **the** Commissary, who gave unmistakable signs of a lively regret at not having been at the masked ball himself, let us off very easily, with a suitable admonition on the danger of quarrelling, calling us *ses enfants*—his children. *Cocher, arrêtez !* "

The coachman stopped as he was ordered; for they were before the peristyle of the Grand Opera.

A noise to which that of Babel let loose would have been comparative silence—a howling, shrieking, leaping, capering, struggling mob—a *tohu-bohu* of extravagant sounds—a whirl of human beings of both sexes arrayed in every variety of incongruous costume—

monks, cavaliers, African kings, Mingrelian princesses, Russian boyards, North American Indians, fishwomen, *débardeurs* and *débardeuses*, marquises, sailors, savages, ballet-dancers, *contadine*, Pierrots, Eastern sultans, negroes, " John Bulls," Jewish Rabbis, field-marshals, fairies, griffins, devils, quack doctors, grenadiers of the First Empire, crusaders, men-at-arms, Punches, *mousquetaires gris*, Highlanders, troubadours, heralds, gipsies, lazzaroni, Queen Elizabeths, Henri Quatres, François Premiers, court jesters, Robert Macaires, old women. and Robinson Crusoes, were all pent up together in the expanse of the boarded *parterre* of the *Académie Impériale de Musique*. But it is not to be assumed, that the whole of the audience were in fancy dresses. A very large proportion—the ladies —were in variously-coloured dominoes; a still larger proportion—the gentlemen—were in plain evening dress, similar to the unpretending attire patronised by Philip Leslie; some wearing masks with lace fall *barbes*, as the French call them; others disdaining even that

transparent disguise, and walking about un-
concernedly, as they would have walked about
the saloons of the Tuileries, or the sky-blue
halls of Almack's in England.

CHAP. XL.

RUN TO EARTH.

PHILIP and his friend went into a private
box on the third tier, and, leaning over
the velvet parapet, contemplated the brilliant
surging scene below. It was some time before
they could accustom their eyes to it, however;
for the respiration of so many thousand
persons, and the glare of the great chandeliers,
lighted with gas, formed an irridescent cloud
that canopied the whole audience, and at first
made it difficult to discern their movements.
So those who have been hardy — perhaps fool-
hardy — enough to take a place in the car of
a balloon, and have risen with the monster

from Cremorne to Vauxhall, haply in the eventide, have seen hanging close over the brow of
the Monster City, and cut justly and exactly
to its shape — to the minutest zigzags of its
outlying suburbs, a great canopy of exhalation
— the smoke of London, hideous and Cim-
merian enough when from *terra firma* we see
it ascending from chimney-pots, or mark its
blackening or destructive effects upon the most
beautiful of our architectural monuments; but
rendered, when seen from heaven, deliciously
azure, viewed as it is through the medium of
a clear and pure atmosphere, and prismatically
glorious by the rays of the setting sun.

The Doctor had provided himself with an
enormous *jumelle* lorgnette, its barrels of
papier maché glistening with japan, mother-of-
pearl enamel, and coloured foil. This instru-
ment completely put to shame Philip's modest
little ivory opera-glass, and vexed the Painter
considerably by its huge size and air of pre-
tension; but Doctor Ionides evidently regarded
it as part and parcel of his equipment, and as
a necessary item of exaggeration to an ex-

aggerated whole. He made good use of it, too, glaring into the brilliant space with the two huge lenses, till the refractions from the facets of the chandelier drops caught his spurious eyes, and made them dance in many-coloured flashes, so that the people in the lower tier must have taken him for a revolving light, or an overgrown basilisk.

"Very good — very good indeed!" the Doctor cried out approvingly.

"What is very good? Who is very good? Do you mean that little figure in the pink domino talking to the man with the counterfeit nose, who appears to have stuffed a chest of drawers, or a bed and bedding, at least, underneath his waistcoat?"

"Quite the contrary! I mean the distinguished individual in evening dress as faultless as yours; but with a mask on, and with the ribbons of half-a-dozen orders at his buttonhole. Pray remark the Legion of Honour, who has just picked the pocket of the man with the false nose. A well-lined purse, evidently."

" The rascal! Shall we go down and collar him?"

" Shall we go down and try to find a needle in a bottle of hay? See! he has already disappeared. I couldn't have done a better trick than that in the days when I was a professor of natural magic. And — ha! ha! — the best of the joke is, that I know the man with the nose and the abdomen. We work together, sometimes. Upon my word, very good—very good, indeed!"

For all his rouge, his wig, his spectacles, you could see his wicked face radiant with the exultation of the cynicism within him. So laugh those horrible, bull-necked, low-browed, square-jowled, small-eyed men in ragged fustian and fur caps, and with blue-and-white-spotted Belchers twisted round their foul throats; so laugh those lost creatures, born irremediably bad; so laugh those hopeless ones born irrevocably STUPID, into whose souls of Erebus not one ray of blessed light shall ever penetrate, let the jail chaplain preach till he be hoarse — the law of kindness be tried to its blandest enactment — the law of severity tried to the last knot in the last cord of its scourge — the law of Draco tried till Calcraft take the wall of Baring and Rothschild, Mirés and Pereire, and bid uncompeted with for the next Russian loan. So laugh the devil's children, who hang about low street corners and lean against Seven Dial posts, when they hear a ribald expression, when they see an animal in torture, when they can stain the clean garments of a passer-by with mud, or overturn the apple-stall of some poor, honest wretch, fighting against starvation like a drowning man against the strong, pitiless sea; so must laugh the devils themselves, grinning at their own damnation—for despair can laugh as well as joy.

Philip looked as sternly as his irresolute eyes would let him at the man-hyæna in the masquerade dress; and it may be that for a moment he mentally discussed the feasibility of lifting his immoral Mentor bodily in his arms, and pitching him over the box-ledge into the merry slough of despond that weltered

underneath, there to find his level of corrup-
tion. But he did not do this: he did very
few things whose feasibility he discussed,
preferring to do those things on the impulse
of the moment, which experience afterwards
proved to be anything but feasible; and when
his companion suggested there was one thing
for which they might really go down stairs
with some show of reason — namely, to take
some refreshment—he allowed Doctor Ionides
to put his arm through his, and to lead him
into the box-lobby, very much in the fashion
that a lamb is led to the slaughter, or as a fool
to the correction of the stocks.

All the lobbies were full of maskers — not
one of them tipsy yet, as their compeers at an
English masquerade would have been two
hours before; but making far more noise over
their goblets of lemonade and overbrimming
bumpers of *orgeat*, their frantic excesses of
candied chocolate, and their Heliogabalian
debauches of sugar-plums, than any like number of Anglo-Saxon Bacchanalians, already
deep in their tenth tumblers of strong toddy,

and making their minds up now to steady drinking. There were noisy girls and noisy young men. There was gabbling, shouting, romping, capering, joking; and all this was thought to be dissipation, the wildest frenzy of carnivalic excitement. So a neophyte might have thought, and so many, doubtless, thought that night, ignorant of how readily sugar-and-water gets into French people's heads, and what a racking headache over-indulgence in barley-sugar will bring on the morning after. But so thought not certain men with tanned, yellow, tired features — men with loose wrinkles hanging flaccidly beneath their eyes and round their hollow cheeks — men in black suits, patent-leather boots — irreproachably-white-cravatted, faultlessly-white-kid-gloved; sometimes wearing moustaches, twisted, waxed, and blackened to painful perfection; frequently having curly heads of hair, which treacherous napes of necks and perfidious partings denounced as wigs instanter — men who looked with a very ill-disguised comtempt upon the tomfooleries of the poor capering *débardeurs*

and *Pierrots*, but from time to time singled
out gliding figures in variously-coloured
dominoes and closely masked, or were singled
out by them; and slipped bits of paper beneath
drapery, or were playfully stricken with fans,
or had their hands squeezed by little fingers
covered with the softest of Jouvin's gloves,
but which little fingers, as I live, belonged to
hands whose grip was as that of a steel vice,
and whose blood-compelling tenacity rivalled
that of an English bull-dog.

"Who is that, I wonder?" Philip asked,
noticing one of the type I have sketched
passing him.

"Am not aware of him," the Doctor
answered; "but know the school well. Lots of
them here. See them in the 'lion's den'—that
long pit proscenium box yonder — on opera
nights, but seldom before the ballet comes on;
see them in the Bois de Boulogne, not like the
young French swells on horses which they
don't know how to ride, but in high tilburies
with English blood-horses which they allow
their grooms to drive for them; see them in

the snug little *baignoires* of the minor theatres,
that is, if your eyes are sharp enough to catch
a sight of them in the obscurity, and of the
princess with the diamond, the big fan, and
the paint, who accompanies them; see them at
Longchamps and Chantilly, at Dieppe in the
summer, after that at the gambling places on
the Rhine. They dine at the Café de Paris;
they think the Trois Frères low; but sometimes condescend to patronise Bignon's or the
Café de Foy, because everything is so very
dear there, and poached eggs with asparagus
tips cost ten francs a plate. They belong to
the Jockey Club; they belong to the Cercle
des Etrangers. You may see them for one
hour, and for one hour only, every day during
the winter season, from four to five, on the
Boulevard des Italiens. At any other time
they are to be found wherever there are expensive wines, ortolans, pâtés de foie gras, and
ladies who call themselves actresses, because
they must call themselves something. Stop!
the atmosphere of playing cards and dice is not
uncongenial to them; neither are duelling
pistols; neither are small swords.''

" You seem to know a great deal about them without telling me their names," Philip said, as threading the crowded passages the Doctor rattled out these physiological remarks; not in one continuous speech, but in detached apophthegms, ever and anon interspersing them with compliments and witticisms, both verbal and manual, addressed to the prettiest of the *débardeurs*, and the most mysterious of the dominoes whom he met, but which I have not deemed necessary to interpolate in my narrative.

" I know them! Bless your heart, I should think I do! I have had to swindle some of them in my time. One famous rendezvous of ours, however, is broken up; there is no Frascati's now, no ' ninety-two ' no ' hundred and fourteen' in the Palais Royal. The cruel Municipality of Paris has killed the gambling-houses; the number of suicides, they say, though I don't believe it, has sensibly diminished; and Othello's occupation, including a very lucrative one of your humble servant, is gone."

" Are these men gamblers, then—black-legs?"

" Gamblers, and rare ones, yes. Blacklegs, no. Not, at least, till they have spent all their money, and can't borrow or win any more without cheating. My dear Phil (Philip shuddered as the diminutive struck his tympanum) these men are the *viveurs de Paris*—the bucks, swells, bloods, dandies, fast men of France. They began under the Restoration. They inherit the traditions of the empire and its wild orgies; they sneer at and despise the frivolous gaiety of the shop-keeping monarchy. These are Russian princes, French nobles of the old *régime*, English lords; yes, I have passed three or four to-night who have inhabited Paris since the year '14; bankers, monster stock-jobbers, generals, and Spanish hidalgoes. They come to a *bal masqué*, as a matter of course; the game they hunt is here too, though you see it not. But the carnival of these worthy souls won't begin till three or four o'clock this morning. There will be no lack of champagne and

screeching then, I promise you; but it will be
between four walls thickly padded. How
thirsty I am to be sure. Suppose we begin
our champagning now."

There was a refreshment-stall, with a mob of
parti-coloured carnivalisers struggling beforeit;
the principal objects of competition being those
large ribbon-bedecked *bâtons* of *sucre de pomme*
—a mysterious species of sweetmeat, into whose
composition sugar and apples enter, I know,
but in what proportions I am not prepared to
say, and which a party of young dandies—
not the mature *viveurs*, you may be sure—
had been simple enough to purchase at the
rate of twenty-five francs the *bâton*, and offer
in a species of scramble among the young
ladies in the silken skirts, the flaxen wigs, the
embroidered caps, and the many-hued velvet
pantaloons; these sticks of *sucre de pomme*
being doubly valuable, not only as pledges of
affection, but as objects of commerce, they
being susceptible, on (private) presentation at
the refreshment counter, of conversion into
cash (by virtue of an occult arrangement

between the confectioner and the *débardeur*),
at a discount of fifty per cent. The Doctor
was pushing his way through this covetously-
saccharine croud, when he suddenly stopped,
and whispered to Philip—

"There he is!"

It was Lord Baddington. Flushed, tum-
bled, somewhat thick in speech, very much
gone in champagne, but a mighty nobleman
still. His Lordship had evidently been
dining; so had his Lordship's toad-eaters, who
were more obsequious than ever, though
somewhat incoherent, not to say drunken in
their flattery.

The young Lord was standing with his
back to the buffet, casting his twenty franc
pieces about in foolish purchases, cramming
ill-reckoned change of five-franc pieces into
his pocket, laughing, swearing, chucking
a little harem of masquerade beauties under
the chin, making a very great noise, ordering
people about, calling the passing French
dandies (very probably as well born, and most
certainly better bred than himself) "cads,"

and otherwise comporting himself in that affably-insolent and condescendingly-ferocious manner not quite uncommon among young British patricians, and which has earned us such a delightful popularity abroad.

" Now's your time," Doctor Ionides laconically observed. " I'll be back in five minutes. Stop! have a drink first, though I don't think you stand much in need of Dutch courage. Don't go in for thrashing him. You see he's screwed, and the French, besides not liking fisticuffs under any circumstances, would call hitting a drunken man cowardly. A fillip by the side of the nose, a tweak of the ear, the slightest flap of a glove, are sufficient. I hope to find you in the thick of it when I return."

He had no sooner spoken than he was gone. Philip, much as he loathed the man, felt disconcerted by his sudden disappearance. He did not know exactly how to act; how to begin the quarrel; what to say, what to do.

He had not long to wait in indecision. He

was looking, I daresay, with a very perturbed expression of countenance at Lord Baddington, when that nobleman was good enough to ask him what the —— he was looking at?"

"I am looking at you," Philip Leslie answered, with as much coolness as he could command, and subduing an impulse to knock the Peer down out of hand. "I want to speak to you, my Lord."

"I thought you were an Englishman," the other answered, essaying to steady himself on his drunken (though noble) legs. "You look so dam like an Englishman." Lord Baddington was in a gracious temper that night.

"Here, Gambroon; Tapetie," he cried out, "here's an Englishman. Haven't I seen you somewhere, old boy—at Crockey's, eh? Let's have a bottle of sham—a bottle of Roiderer's best, hay? No; what I am going to—that is what—yes, what are you going to stand?"

"Nothing," Philip answered. "Come here, I tell you. I want to speak to you. Do you know the name on this card?"

He put a card into his hand, with his own name, Leslie, upon it. But Lord Baddington, regarding it with a hazy stare, shook his head from side to side, with an air of the wisest folly, or the most imbecile wisdom; and again stating his opinion that Philip was a good fellow, and one of the right sort, suggested shandy-gaff, and that they should call the waiter in to spar.

"If you are too drunk to read, you are sober enough to hear," answered Philip fiercely. "My name, Lord Baddington, is Leslie — Philip Leslie. Do you understand now?"

"Well, Mr. Meslie, and what the doose is that to me!"

He fell back as he said so, however, doubtful and puzzled in his look, and pressing his hand on his hot forehead, as if to recall some bygone thought or thing. The masquers had partly given way before them, partly elbowed them into a corner, and they were comparatively alone in a grove of drinking flasks, artificial flowers, and glass jars full of cakes and sweetmeats.

"I am Philip Leslie," the Artist repeated slowly and sternly.

The Peer suddenly started; with a half reel and a half scream, cried out:

"—— you, you're that painter fellow; you're the low-life cad who——"

"I am the man who, never having harmed you by word or deed, you have yet grossly, basely, villanously injured. I am he who was to have been the husband of the girl whom you have taken away in your high and mighty caprice to make a plaything of—to cast her away when you have done with her. Give me back my wife, Lord Baddington!"

But Lord Baddington stood looking at him with a scared fixedness, as though he had been some horrible image—Medusa's head— a chimera—the ghost of Banquo—the skull of murdered John Hayes, stuck on a pole in St. Margaret's Churchyard, Westminster; but not a word spake he. The toadies, flurried, and (one of them) frightened, hovered about, hearing all, and skirmished off another group of masquers that had begun to gather.

"You *cannot* give her back to me," the Painter continued, " not as I—as any honest man—could desire to receive her. You have ruined her, scoundrel as you are. Do you hear me, my Lord,—scoundrel?"

He heard, but answered never a syllable. The toadies winced at the word scoundrel, and made ready for the worst. Philip grew impatient as he proceeded—

" You can give me one thing, at least: the satisfaction of a gentleman—revenge. I give this card to one of your friends, since you are not in a state to comprehend its meaning yourself. My address is on it; but I will be under the orchestra at the conclusion of the ball, if you can take enough soda-water by that time to sober yourself by that time, and answer me."

He tendered his card as he spoke to Major Gambroon, and was walking away like a man of snow, very cool without, though very warm within, when Lord Baddington called out "Stop," and took the card himself from the hand of his friend.

A most remarkable change had come over this nobleman. He could not have sobered himself in so short a time, violent as might have been the revulsion of feeling he had experienced; but he began to speak quite lucidly and coherently, putting his face close to Philip's, and glaring at him with baleful eyes.

"I won't fight you," he said. "That yellow-haired cat in Curzon Street has sent you here to murder me. I won't fight you. I'm no coward. Curse me if I'm a coward; but I won't be murdered. Go back to London. Go back to that young hag. Go to the devil."

He crushed the card into a ball, and flung it into Philip's face; then turned towards his toadies with a yell half of cowardice, half of defiance. But the next moment, a well-directed blow from the painter caused him to measure his length upon the ground.

CHAP. XLI.

LORD BADDINGTON SUPS AND BREAKFASTS.

IT was not through any feeling of pusil-
lanimity that Pollyblank-Ionides—Captain,
Professor, and Doctor —· had abandoned his
friend under what may appear to have been
critical circumstances. Cowardice was not
certainly one of that outlaw's failings; and
though, like the majority of valiant men, who
are also prudent, he recognised to its fullest
extent the valuable expediency of running
away under certain circumstances — a similar
retrograde policy having been occasionally
practised with the utmost success by the most
illustrious commanders — the multi-named
companion of Philip Leslie was, when need

required it, a *chevalier*, if not exactly *sans re-proche*, decidedly one *sans peur*.

The Doctor's organ of locality was power-fully developed, and he knew to a cubic foot, a cubic inch, where he had left Philip. But he had a visit to pay before he rejoined him; and from the manner, while he traversed the crowd, in which he kept his gaze fixed on a certain box on the ground-tier — a small pit-box — it might not unreasonably be conjec-tured that he had an *affaire de cœur* in that neighbourhood. He was a gay man, Doctor Ionides; but he was not, for the moment, very popular among the sex, as he strode towards his destination; for he elbowed the *débardeurs* and *titis* mercilessly, and broke into and through so many couples and figures of the mazy dance, that he was at last pursued by yells of Terpsichorean execration; nay, on one or two occasions, the Municipal Guards in attendance manifested signs of giving him chase, and bringing him to condign punish-ment, for his infraction of the laws of *cavalier seul* or *chasser-croiser;* but either he was

nimble enough to escape the police Nemesis,
or it may be, his towering plume and stalwart
limbs dismayed the diminutive alguazils, or —
and this is the most probable theory of all —
the police were, like all true Frenchmen, too
much absorbed in the delirious excitement of
the saltatory evolutions, to pay attention to a
transient interruption.

The Doctor passed up one of the inclined
planes, covered with crimson cloth, leading to
the box lobbies, entered one of those *couloirs*,
and knocked at the door of box No. 9. He
had to knock twice, and then the door was
timidly opened. Inverting the action of Margaret Douglas, in Scott's immortal tale, who
used her arm as a bolt, in order that a door
might remain closed, Doctor Ionides took advantage of the door not being a door, but
rather a-jar, to use his arm as a wedge, and,
by rapidly thrusting it through the narrow
aperture, secured the door's remaining open.
Then, by an agile movement of his foot, he
widened the opening; soon found himself
inside the box; closed the door after him;

put a chair against it; turned nimbly on his feet; seized a light chair in his strong grasp; deftly sat himself down thereupon; turned towards a closely-masked domino, who was crouching in a corner, and affectionately accosted Manuelita the dancing-girl, who, half dead with terror, was trembling now with her wrist in his grasp, and his flaming face leering under the black lace valance of her mask. The satyr had seized the poor little dryad; the linnet was in the clutches of the hawk.

"Who are you?" she gasped.

"I am Bogey," playfully answered the Doctor. "The sweep—the black man—the beadle—the policeman. I was Professor Jachimo who was so fond of you in Liverpool; always fond of you, my charming little Manuelita. Good Professor Jachimo—clever Professor Jachimo—funny Professor Jachimo. Now I'm Doctor Ionides, quite as good, clever, and funny; and if you speak a word above your breath, you little minx, I'll wring your neck for you first, and cut your throat afterwards."

She tried to scream; but her respiration

scarcely fluttered the cobweb-lace that guarded
her lips. Her little pulse trotted like the feet
of a mouse running away to its hole. She felt
as though a swoon, tears, hysterics, death,
would have been a relief; but she was fas-
cinated by the garish phantom before her, and
could not move. At last she whispered :

" You come from Philip?"

" Not the least in the world, my little pet,"
The Doctor urbanely rejoined. " I am my
own ambassador, town-traveller, gentleman-
usher, master of the ceremonies, and everything else included; and I come from myself,
and I want you to come with me."

" With you," she murmured; " with you,
bad and cruel man !"

" If you *don't*," the Doctor explained; "if
you don't take my arm this very moment, and
walk down stairs with me, I'll tell you what
will happen. Shall I tell you ?"

She could not answer; she could only look
at him.

" Silence gives consent. I'll tell you. Unless you obey me, by six o'clock this morning

—it's one now—your duck-of-diamonds, your handsome soldier-officer, your fair-haired dandy of a lord, shall be a bleeding corpse—dead, dead as a leg of Welsh mutton, my dear, and with a small sword through his heart."

" Would you murder him ?"

" That's my business; I only tell you what will take place. I never forget, never forgive anything. if you obey me, you shall come to no harm, and you will save his life. If you refuse, you must take the consequences. Now, are you ready?"

She rose up tottering, and put her flaccid arm in his. Why should she believe him, this convicted, perjured liar and cheat ? She believed in him less, perhaps, for his dire threats, and horrible presence, and power of terrifying, than because she *loved* the bad man who had taken her away. Find me a woman who really loves a man, and I will go to her without introduction and without credentials, and if I tell her he whom she loves is in danger or distress, I will make her do anything I choose, from dancing a saraband to pawning her earrings.

He led her into the lobby. A whiskered French dandy, with a white waistcoat, and white cravat so enormous in their dimensions, and with such little black doeskin legs, that he looked like a portrait of Mr. Allbody, came up to her to whisper some conventional, stereotyped *bal masqué* compliment in her ear. But before he had half got through the expression of his opinion that she was a Mingrelian princess, and that she was *adorablement belle* that evening, the dexterous Doctor administered to him such an elphantine stamp on one of his varnished feet, and such a catapultean blow with the elbow in his white-vested ribs, that the Frenchman was yet screeching with pain, and spluttering out a preliminary *sacre*, when the Doctor had divided the crowd, and was beneath the portico in the Rue Lepelletier.

There was as great a crowd without as within, but a black crowd, illumined here and there by the glare of a gas-lamp. In the roadway mounted gendarmes pranced and cursed to keep the people back, and the confusion of coaches and coachmen was awful.

"This way," the Doctor said, briefly.

It was the turning point. The girl hung back for a second. Had she screamed, had she resisted, rescue was certain. There were hundreds of policemen round about her. But she dared not. She thought of the man she loved being foully, cruelly murdered, and she obeyed.

A little *voiture de remise*, with two horses, was drawn up close between the last two pillars to the right of the portico. The door of this carriage was open, and there was an attendant lacquey, in the shape of a long man in a very long great coat, a worsted comforter with long straggling ends about his neck, and a very tall hat. He did not look much like a footman. On the box was a fat man in a cap, who looked even less like a coachman. Manuelita noticed both these little circumstances with the momentary microscopic power terror awakens in us.

"Number twelve," cried the Doctor, thrusting, rather than helping, Manuelita into the carriage.

" *Numero douze*," the long man grumbled, bundling himself into the carriage too.

" *Numero* ——" the fat coachman seemed to be muttering; but whether it were twelve or twelve hundred thousand he meant, matters little; for in another instant a whip was flourished, the horses plunged, the carriage was gone, ploughing up the raging crowd, while Doctor Ionides stood under the peristyle with his arms akimbo, and laughed, Ha! ha!

" A clean trick, cleanly done," he chuckled. "If she had squeaked it would have been awkward. I think two inside can manage her. Escargotier has had rougher customers than she, poor little doll; and as to Sacripandot, he could master the Dragon of Wantley."

He had done his ministering very quickly, if not very gently, and the whole abduction— if abduction it were—of Manuelita had been effected in something under seven minutes. He strode back into the theatre. There is a law prohibiting re-admission of masquers at the Grand Opera; yet somehow Doctor Ionides passed unquestioned, and he reached that refreshment counter already known to you, just as a great shout arose among the bystanders that *deux Anglais se boxaient*—that two Englishmen were fighting.

Baddington, felled to the earth, was still an old public-school boy, and though just before by implication a coward in refusing to fight Philip, he was roused and sobered, as most Englishman are, however far gone, and when not stunned, by a blow. He no longer saw before him the minister of his grand-aunt's vengeance. He simply saw before him a man who had knocked him down, and whom it was desirable to kill with his fists, if possible. He was up again in a moment, and closed with Philip. Both were strong, active, young, well set men. One had the advantage of perfect sobriety, but he was enraged; to the other, . partial intoxication lent increase of rage, augmentation of strength. The mob around them grew thicker and thicker, the police were said to be coming up, when Doctor Ionides, burst through the throng, and with two movements of his big arms—one the movement of a swimmer plunging, the other that of the sails of a windmill when the wind is fresh — separated the combatants.

" I'll knock both of you down if you ain't quiet," he cried in his great excitement. " The bobbies will be here in a second. *La police a l'œil sur nous. Soyez tranquille, mes enfants.* Come away Phil; and you, Mr. What's-his-name, take your man away, and let me talk to the other—he looks like a fire-eater."

Mr. Tapetie led away Lord Baddington, who now began to relapse into something very like stupidity again; but it must be admitted that the *attaché* looked as though he would most devoutly have wished that he could take himself away instead of his friend. Major Gambroon, pleased perhaps at the appellation of fire-eater, perchance delighted at the prospect, however remote, of a duel, crossed amicably over to Doctor Ionides, who, base-born, vulgar, and disreputable as he undoubtedly was, appeared undoubtedly at that moment the master of the situation.

" One moment, Mr.——, and then we will go to business," he said. " I have a word to speak to my friend."

The Major bowed, and handed him his card.

" Major Gambroon; ha, delighted, I'm sure. United Service Club, I see. Here's my card. Sorry I don't belong to any club save one at Grand Cairo, and as I haven't paid my subscription for ten years, I suppose I'm scratched."

The Major took the card, and looked at it with somewhat of a puzzled countenance; but he bowed again notwithstanding.

" Now, Philip," the Doctor whispered, " I want you to be a good boy and do as I tell you. Will you promise to keep yourself quiet—I'll get the enemy away—and meet me under the clock of the orchestra at four precisely. You shall shoot your foe, I'll promise you that; and, on my word and honour—I have a word and honour somewhere—you shall have some good news of Manuelita."

" You do not mean to say that?" Philip eagerly exclaimed.

"I mean to say that you must do what I ask you. Will you?"

"Yes."

"Then be off with you. Go and dance, sing, eat bon-bons, make love, drink champagne —only not too much — anything you like, till four. I'll arrange everything."

He watched Philip, with a cunning twinkle in his bad eyes, as the painter strutted away into the midst of the harlequinade, lost in thought.

"A good lad, that," said Doctor Ionides to himself; "with plenty of stuff in him. It's a pity he hasn't more muscle of mind. I think I like him better than anybody else in the world, *bar one*, and yet I am afraid I shall be obliged to bring him to a bad end. Now, Major Gambroon, I am at your service."

*   *   *   *   *

There were things done in Paris that night and morning, at which the very stones should have cried out, the sky should have wept tears of blood. There were ghastly orgies, ghastlier for their splendour; there were the seeds of hatred, and jealousy, and misery, and poverty, and robbery, and violence, and death, sown before the fiddlers who had fiddled the last quadrille were asleep on their pallets in their mean attics.

There was this done in the gray of the winter's morning, and in a lonely *carrière*, a glade of the wood of Vincennes, whose record the Accusing Angel took straightway up on high, and saw it written in red letters — for it was Murder. Two men in ball-dress met, accompanied by four others variously attired, but one of whom had a gilt cuirass under his cloak. Paces were measured, stop watches were opened, a handkerchief was dropped; and as the church clock of Vincennes struck eight, there lay on the bloody snow one of these men in ball-dress, a tall, young, fair stalwart man, his face downwards, and shot to death.

CHAP. XLII.

EIGHTEEN HUNDRED AND FORTY-FIVE.

TEN years. Time to make a fortune, to be beggared, to grow gray, to write *eques* after one's name. Time to be in the commission of the peace or the liberties of the Fleet —if there were a Fleet, or liberties thereunto, now. Time to have a patent of nobility, or a ticket-of-leave. Time enough to die.

Ten years! Ten years is an age. Ten years is the last generation—or the next. Ten years ago we went gipsying; Plancus was consul; times were better, things were different—we were twenty-one, and lived in a garret, and were happy in it. We believed in love and pantomimes; we listened with credulity to the whispers of fancy, and pursued with eagerness the phantoms of hope, believing that age would fulfil the promises of youth, and that the deficiencies of to-day would be made up by to-morrow, and not caring to be told anything about the history of Rasselas, Prince of Abyssinia. Ten years ago we were rich in verdant pastures, corn-lands, even as Squire Boaz that saw Ruth and Naomi come a-gleaning. Now we have stubble on our chins, and corns upon our toes, putting our trust mainly in Mr. Eisenberg. I have often thought, that were I not chained to this pen, as Guzman de Alfarache was to his oar, that if I could put money in my purse, and get a foreign office passport through the kindness of the banking firm where I have that large balance lying (I shall surely want a Pickford's van or a Panic to carry it away some day)— could I only obtain a passport *viséd* for every-where, I should like to go away for ten years —travelling anywhere; sedulously refraining from the perusal of newspapers and period-icals, English or foreign; eschewing even

" Galignani " and the " Cornhill Magazine;" conversing with no men save waiters, barbers, shepherds, and flower-maidens; comporting myself, *enfin*, like a Timon of Athens in broadcloth, lapidating Apemanthus mercilessly if he came to bore me, and turning up my nose at Alcibiades, his womankind, his drums and his fifes; and then, the lustre out, come straightway back to London Bridge, to see how the English world was wagging, and what had become of all my friends. How many were dead, and how many were married? Who had emigrated to New Zealand and had been scraped to death with oyster-shells, or sociably eaten by beat of tom-tom at a palaver among the aborigines? How many were in Parliament, and how many in the " Gazette?" Who among those who were once prompt to borrow the lowly shilling, and not too proud to accept the twice-worn coat, had made large fortunes, and lived in Belgravia? Who of those who were wont to play Amphitryon to me, and chide me if I kept the bottle standing, were blear-eyed and rheumy-lipped, quite old and broken, in St. Pancras Workhouse, or else starched teeto-tallers, talking of the irreparable injury inflicted on the coats of the stomach by the consumption of a glass of Bucellas? How many conceited young pretenders had burst like bubbles, and withered and grown haggard with too much toad-eating, had gone through the Insolvent Court, bid a forced adieu to fine houses, grand company, and the Grimaldi Club, and subsided into shabby clerks, to potato salesmen, and rusty-elbowed commission agents travelling in coals and corn? How many of the dear girls I know now, smiling and blushing in their innocent angling for that which Nature bids them fish for— sweethearts — were become portly matrons, rosy mothers of chubby little Gracchi, and intent no more on flower shows or St. Barnabas' church services, but absorbed in the vital question of the lancing of Alfred's gums, and grave with the responsibility of having Totty's ears pierced? I should like to go away so, for ten years, and, coming back, find you,

Eugenio, a millionnaire; and you, Saccharissa, full of maternal cares; and you, chivalrous descendant of the Douglas and the Bruce, pitching into Government from the Opposition benches of the Commons (having just refused a junior Lordship of the Treasury, an Irish stipendiary magistracy, and the Governorship of Cape Coast Castle, successively offered by a despairing whipper-in): and you, Robert, still driving "the wain of life" (with nuggets in the boot); and you—not " Blithe Carew," but intimate enemy of mine, hanged. Dear friends and readers, if I go away so, or am called, may these ten years lie lightly on your heads: the golden days be merry, the silver days be few. There, bah! I forgive the intimate enemy even—poor shallow rogue. I don't want him to be hanged, the losel, worsted-stocking knave, and be hanged to him!

Look forward to the ten; it is good to do so. Cry out, " Excelsior!" and climb up three hundred and sixty-five better and better steps a year. Look forward, but not back— not back. Remember Lot's wife. Look not upon the old love-letters, the old love locks, the old quarrels, the old hatreds, the old opportunities missed, the old days of happiness gone, never to return. Look not back at high noon Only, in the night season, rise up, when the moon shines very brightly, and the willows whisper their secrets to the secretive pool beneath, that drinks all in and answers not a word; wrap thy cloak about thee, and steal to the place of the tombs, and weep over those who lie in peace, and whom no man can sue now, no woman vex, no anger move. Thou shalt look back then—yea, into the dimmest recesses of the most distant mountains of thy soul-scape, and the angels shall keep the secret of thy retrospect.

*   *   *   *

Ten years had elapsed since the events narrated in the forty-first chapter of this history. London was still the great city; but the time was Eighteen hundred and forty-five, and another king had arisen which knew not Joseph. A king, say I? A gracious lady, rather, who had come seven years before, a timid, blushing girl, to take possession of the throne of silly, white-headed, good King William, and corpulent, curly-wigged, bad King George. "V. R." flourished over all the post-office letter-boxes and on all the police-vans. It was Victoria, not William, by the grace of God, who sent you greeting now, and commanded you that within eight days you entered an appearance before Thomas Lord Denman at Westminster; it was her Majesty the Queen who went to open Parliament in the gingerbread coach, drawn by the cream-coloured horses; and it was her Majesty Queen Victoria, that the play-house managers cried God save, in the Latin language, what time they took the liberty of informing the public that no babies in arms would be admitted, and no money returned.

One August afternoon, in the year Eighteen hundred and forty-five, an old woman was crouching over the fire—though the weather was passing hot—in the little back parlour of a shop in Windmill Street, Tottenham Court Road.

I don't wish to say anything disrespectful
of this elderly female, or to prejudice you in
the outset against her—perish such an ungal-
lant and unjust thought; but I should be
sinning against veracity were I to disguise the
fact, that she was about the ugliest old lady
that you could wish to meet on an autumnal
afternoon, or that you would *not* like the
adored wife of your bosom, who is in delicate
health just now, to meet on any day, or in any
season whatever, under any circumstances at
all.   Neither, I hope, will it be libelling the
venerable individual crouching over the fire,
to hint that if she had lived in the days of
King James the First, of blessed memory, the
odds upon her being arraigned at the very
next assize of Oyer and Terminer as a witch
would have been very heavy, and the chances
of her escape from the faggot and the fire
very slender indeed.   She was, indeed, such a
weird and uncomfortable-looking old woman
to view; and had she, in the present year of
grace even, inhabited some sequestered village
in some cross-country between two lines of

railway, she would, I am persuaded, have been feared as a witch, hated as a witch, conciliated and consulted as a witch, and hooted — perchance pelted — by the village children as a witch. The village blacksmith would have driven a brisk trade in horse-shoes, in connection with the terror inspired by her preternatural appearance; the village baker would have made crosses in the dough if she happened to pass his shop at kneading time. She would have been suffered near no hen-roost, no butter-churn, no beer-barrel. Housewives would have made impromptu crucifixes with scissors laid on chairs at her approach; and superstitious farmers would have attributed the botts in their cattle, the smut in their wheat, and the rheumatism in themselves, to her maleficent powers. She was a very horrible-looking old woman indeed, to say the least. She might have been the great-great-grand-daughter of the Witch of Endor, or a twin-sister of Mademoiselle le Normand, or Megæra come to settle in the neighbourhood of Tottenham Court Road; or

La Mère Croquemitaine, or the late Caliban's mamma, Sycorax, or the Old Woman of Berkeley, or Mother Redcap. She was one of those old ladies who are called "Goody," apparently because they look so very like "Baddy"; and she was an uncommonly ogglesome sight to see.

Ten thousand wrinkles ploughed that yellow face, as dried up watercourses do a high mountain. Little trees grew here and there on that unlovely plain in the shape of tufts of white hair. Shards, and flints, and scoriæ of pimples were thrown up here and there; but the substructure was volcanic; and the red, twinkling eyes were craters, and flamed. A nose and chin that met; a yellow fang or two protruding from the puckered lip; a mop of hideous hair —half white, half wolfish red—straggling from beneath a foul nightcap; a bandage of flannel—new in its texture from its raw blue tinge, but intolerably dirty—passed beneath her chin, as though she were a corpse, and this was to tie up her jaw withal; pendulous cheeks, and flaccid rolls of skin, so hanging about her neck that she might have been an octogenarian *crétin* with a *goître:* these made up—and you require nothing more, I hope— the *ensemble* of her head. She was immensely old, and bowed, and crooked. Her hands were yellow, skinny, and long, with bony fingers, armed with talons rather than nails, and the whole tesselated with designs in dirt. She was pinned up in crasseous rags, rather than clothed. She appeared to have elephantiasis in her feet, so huge appeared they, swathed in bandages and list shoes; and the most dreadful thing about this old woman was, that she appeared to have a perpetual palsy, and shook like a jelly of some foul gelatinous matter, or like a blasted tree whose roots are rotten.

The shop in whose back-parlour this old woman sat, was not an old curiosity shop, nor a chandler's shop, nor a rag shop, nor an old clothes shop, nor a shop whose staple stock-in-trade consisted of old metal and bones. It certainly could not be called a milliner and dressmaker's; it was a long way off being a toy shop; and though dresses, rich and *bizarre*,

abounded on its shelves, it was neither a masquerade warehouse nor a theatrical costumier's.
It was a shop not much bigger than a bird-
cage, sweltering with an amalgamation of all
of all the attributes of all the shops to which
I have called attention. It was a shop em-
phatically of odds and ends, of shreds and
patches, of waifs and strays, of unconsidered
trifles, of sweepings and fragments, and bits,
and rubbish, and treasures. It was a mouldy,
musty, and ineffably mysterious shop, and
there are hundreds like it in London.

The shop was full of secrets; and there
were more romances of the aristocracy on its
dusty shelves than ever Sir Bernard Burke
dreamt of. There were rich silks and brocades
here that a half spilt glass of wine, a speck of
sauce from a butter-boat, a drop of wax from
a taper, had banished from the Queen's palace
and the " nobility's concerts," and had relegated to the Road of Tottenham. There were
ostrich feathers, somewhat dim and jaundiced
now, and coiffures of bird of paradise and
marabout plumes, that had waved over the

fair heads of England's fairest, noblest daughters, or bedizened the turbans of the haughtiest of dowagers, with as many creases in their chins as they had quarterings in their scutcheons. There were sweeping mantles of rich silk velvets that had fallen into voluptuous folds on the cushions of the carriages of duchesses, but which were destined ere long to sweep the floors of casinos, and to be degraded by the mud of the Haymarket. There were gauzy bonnets, glistening with silver sprigs and artificial flowers, through which, however, the dull wire and coarse buckram began to peep, like the copper in the salver whose edges only are of silver, like the flesh of the beggar's knee through his torn trousers. There were tiny satin shoes, with blackened soles and soiled insteps. There were pink silk stockings by dozens frayed over the instep, wofully in want of darning. There were fribbles and frabbles of lace, falling into rich raggedness; bronze kid boots cracked in the upper-leathers; muffs, and boas, and pelerines of costly fur, where the moth had imitated the ringworm's part; bridal veils, from which the silver embroidery had been rudely stripped; white kid gloves, soiled and split, in piles; sashes and scarves, tippets and collars, ivory fans with broken joints, dressing-cases minus the silver tops to the bottles, jet bracelets, velvet reticules, embroidered parasols with torn fringe and no handles, smelling-bottles with no stoppers, lace pocket-handkerchiefs with burns through the centre; all sorts of rich woman's ware, purple fine linen, goldsmith's ware and lace—the whole mixed up with a chaos of sheets and blankets, coarse jean stays, flannels, nightcaps, tablecloths, pillow cases, black cotton stockings, patchwork counter-panes, linsey-woolsey jackets, and huge bundles bursting with undeniable rags. And there was a musty, acrid, vapid odour hanging about the place, similar to that which pervades a pawnbroker's shop in a low neighbourhood on Saturday night, or that department of a jail where the prisoners' outer-world clothes are kept. A big dog, that had once been white, but was now of no particular hue save that of dirt — a wall-eyed dog, irremediably mangy, with a chronic cough, and a settled hatred to his tail, kept watch and ward in the outer shop, sitting by preference on a Marseilles quilt with a great russet-brown stain which looked horribly like blood upon it, and blinking lazily at one solitary ray of the golden autumnal light, which, in a laudable pursuit of polarisation under difficulties, worthy of all commendation, was fighting its way into the shop against the million motes of dust, and the foggy miasma of the place.

In the room—1 don't like to call it hole, for fear of being thought rude —where the old woman crouched, there were more shelves, more bundles, more treasures in rags, more odds and ends. There was a portrait, too, of the lamented and injured Caroline of Brunswick, sometime Queen of England—a vile mezzotinto thing in a tawdry frame, and screened by a glass, cracked and smoky, representing that Royal Personage in the act of receiving an address from the ladies of England (with very short waists and enormous hats

and feathers), at Brandenburg House, near
Hammersmith. There was a monster of a
parrot in a battered cage — a moulting brute,
with a broken wing, plumage of sooty green,
and a diabolical head, with eyes like the
danger-lights of a locomotive—which shrieked,
and croaked, and swore, and blasphemed, and
swung himself on his rusty ring, like a Prophet
of Evil or a bird possessed by a demon. The
walls of the room — where there were no
shelves — were plastered thickly over with
placards relating to sales by auction, chiefly
of pawnbrokers' unredeemed pledges; the floor
was littered with torn catalogues from Oxen-
ham's, and Debenham and Storr's sale-rooms;
and on the ricketty table, amid a heap of rags,
stay-busks, lace-cuffs, halfpence, candle-ends,
and remnants of cloth and silk, there were
some hundreds — there could not have been
less — of little quadrangular scraps of pasteboard, bent, dirty, torn, inkstained, and pin-
punctured, which the experienced eye would
have no difficulty in recognising at once as
pawnbrokers' duplicates. Pardon the verbosity

of this description.   The frame was as necessary as the picture; the setting as the jewel.
And there is one thing, too, which I have forgotten in my inventory; this — that over the
outer door of the shop — which was a remarkably villanous-looking shop, by-the-way, and
offered no better *étalage* than bundles and
lace-rags— in the street there was this inscription — " Mrs. Tinctop.   Ladies' Wardrobes
purchased."

Mrs. Tinctop — I scorn to deceive you —
was the proprietor of the shop where the
ladies' wardrobes were purchased; and Mrs.
Tinctop — I am above hypocrisy, I hope —
was Mr. Tinctop's mamma — that Mr. Tinctop
with whom you have been made acquainted,
more or less, almost since the commencement
of this chronicle; and, finally, Mrs. Tinctop
was the veritable old lady who was crooning
over the fire.

The wall-eyed dog that took care of the
outer premises gave an asthmatic growl, which
ended in a squeak, as the shop-door opened,
causing at the same time an ill-conditioned

tinkle on a cracked bell; and there walked in, as stealthily as of yore, Mr. Seth Tinctop, general practitioner.

A little balder, a little more weazened as to countenance, a little stouter in figure, but the same smooth, urbane Seth Tinctop still. He had mounted gold-rimmed spectacles and gone into goloshes; he carried a plump silk umbrella, and wore a substantial watch-chain. The ten years seem to have been prosperous years, to have used him well, and to have done him good.

He bestowed a subdued whistle of recognition upon the dog, who immediately either acknowledged or resented that act of courtesy, by making a furious onslaught upon his stump of a tail. Then Mr. Tinctop walked through the miasma of decayed millinery into the hole where his mamma dwelt, and, with another whistle, to which was superadded a nod, sat himself down over against her by the fireside.

" Good afternoon, mother."

These people do say " good afternoon," " good morning," " good-bye," and " good night," just as we Christians do. They are human — they are mortal. Williams set his children to play with the Italian boy before he murdered him for the sake of his white teeth. If you pinch a thief, he will cry out; if you prick a rascal, he will bleed; if you tickle him, he will laugh. The robbers of the Rhine are not always accoutred in slouched hats and buff-boots, and swaggering about with Snickasnees. They put on carpet-slippers at eventide, smoke their pipes at the ingle-nook, kiss their wives, and when they go to bed, put on nightcaps with tassels and strings that tie underneath the chin.

CHAP. XLIII.

TO PARISH CLERKS AND OTHERS.

A S in a wood fire that has been neglected, and where the logs, raging hot within, are one uniform ashen grey without, one whisper of the bellows will illumine the dull hearth with a ruddy glow, send the red sparks scintillating up the chimney, and set the logs themselves flaming; so the filial salutation addressed by Mr. Tinctop to his mother seemed to light up the hitherto extinguished countenance of that ancient dame — to kindle the fire of life in those vacuous eyes — to change her from an exact counterpart of an Egyptian mummy to an indifferent imitation of a live old woman. She began to get up

from her chair in a doddering, scrambling
way, and wagged her old jaws amicably at her
son, who sate himself down over against her
on a species of beggar's throne, made up of
rags, bundles, the fragments of an arm-chair,
a plank or two, and a horse-hair sofa pillow.
Then he took a long clay pipe from a sort of
cave of Trophonius of cobwebs and cracked
crockery ware high up in the wall beyond the
mantelpiece, filled it with tobacco, lighted it
gravely, and began to smoke it demurely,
looking very precise and proper and profes-
sional, and quite as though he were in possession of all due certificates of having passed the
Hall of Apothecaries and the College of
Surgeons, and not at all like Bamfylde Moore
Carew, which renowned King of Beggars he
should in all consistency, considering the place
he was in and the company he kept, have
looked like.

The old woman tottered to another cupboard, opened it, hunted among its shelves to
the apparent discomposure of a colony of rats
which, by the quadrupedental pattering noise

heard, it may be presumed resided there, and at last produced an inconceivably dirty stone bottle, which might possibly at some remote period of time have been used as an amphora for Day and Martin's blacking; which, from some pearly drops of congealed adipose matter about the neck, appeared to have served at one stage of its career as an impromptu candlestick; and which now might have been taken as a receptacle for snuff, or turpentine, or mixed pickles, or furniture stuff, or mixture to kill cockroaches. From it, however, Mrs. Tinctop poured a semi-transparent liquid into a battered pewter measure, popped thereinto a lump of sugar, which she produced from the recesses of a faded blue ball — a napkin I hope, a pocket-handkerchief I fear — and filled the measure up with boiling water from a hopelessly-battered and rusty copper kettle, with a tin lid, a frayed rope handle like that to a gipsy's plunder-pot, and a drooping nozzle twisted all awry. Whatever the whitish liquid may have been, it seemed to be something good to drink, and as Mr. Tinctop drank it, it seemingly did him good too, for he smacked his thin lips, and his narrow, bald forehead shone again.

To the great delight of his mamma, who went and stroked the said bald *os frontis*, smoothing the spare locks, and gazing with inexpressible fondness into his eyes.

" Does your pipe draw, deary ?" she asked coaxingly.

Trivial and absurd, and sordid as the question was, there was a profundity of solicitude in it, and made it, comparatively, superior to an inquiry as to whether Mr. Tinctop had the contents of the mines of Golconda in his waistcoat pocket, whether he had the paradise of Mahomet at his command, or whether he felt as happy as the Grand Turk.

" Pretty well, mother," answered Mr. Tinctop.   " You might keep your snuff out of my tobacco.   I don't mind the pepper; that gives it a flavour; but one can't smoke and sneeze at once comfortably.   Where do you get your whiskey?"

" Round the corner, deary."   She pointed

her skinny thumb over her shoulder and into
the dim obscurity of a corner. Where that
may have been — in the Land of Nod, or in
the kingdom of Cockaigne — anywhere, or
nowhere — this deponent sayeth not.

"The next time you get fourpenn'orth,"
remarked her son, "tell them not to put
poison in it. It interferes with the trade in
drugs. How's business, mother? — lively?
plenty coming in, eh?"

"I ain't got no money, Seth," the old
woman exclaimed with a sort of feeble scream.
"I ain't, indeed. I can't get none. Not a
blessed copper, not a ha'penny, my son."
And as she spoke she folded her shrivelled
arms tightly, drawing her tottering knees
together, and screwing her head on one side,
with blinking eyes, and trembling lips, like a
magpie at bay, looking into a marrowbone and
determined to defend it.

"Who the deuce wants your money?"
Mr. Tinctop called out testily. "You're
always squalling out about your money, you
covetous old woman, you. I don't want your

money. I've plenty of my own. I only asked you how business was."

"Bad! Bad! Bad!" his mother mumbled, in reply. "No money to be got, Seth dear ——"

"Money again!" interrupted her exasperated son. "I do believe you think of nothing but money. Did I ask you for any? Do I ever have any from you?"

"Not now, not now, deary!" the old woman said hastily. "But you've had a deal — oh a deal o' money from me, you know, ducky. You'll have it all when I die—all when I die, darling; but you must wait — yes, wait — wait a bit. Times are so hard, you know."

"She's doting. She's half silly. She's a confounded old idiot!" Mr. Tinctop, neither very courteously nor very dutifully, grumbled to himself. "Hark ye, mother," he said aloud; "do you want to *get* some more money?"

The weazened face, which was fast sinking into vacuity, lighted up again at the magic word. Eyes red with the concupiscence of gain shone out of the darkness like glowworms. She was all huddled, and excited, and tumultuous in her chair, and babbled out some toothy assurances of how much she liked money, and the grand things she would do for her darling Seth, if he would only put her in the way of making some.

"Then just tell me who has been here this morning?" Mr. Tinctop said, laying down his pipe. "That's what I meant when I asked you how business was."

"Let's see — let's see!" the old woman answered. "I'll tell you, Seth. First, there was the Bishop's man, which his Lordship's not expected to live. He brought an a'pn and a shovel 'at, and nine o' the beautifullest cambric shirts you ever see. Long shirts they was, too, a'most as long as night gownds."

"Anybody else?"

"Old Sally from the square brought some fat, kitchen-stuff, and sich like."

"What! mother; do you deal in dripping? I suppose you give the best price for rags and bones, too. Why don't you hang out a black doll over the door?"

"It's all very well laughing at an old 'ooman like me," his mother retorted in some dudgeon; "but I know my bisness as well as most people. I don't deal in rags and bones, Mister Seth; but I buy drippin', Mister Seth — 'tickulary when there's a silver spoon or two in it, and a malacky brooch — you know one of those green ones — in it; and p'raps a bran new pair o' fur cuffs, and a beautiful skyblue pairasol. Aha! what d'ye think o' drippin' and black dolls now!"

She held her head forward, grinning and chattering in a manner half ominous and half demoniacal, very terrific to behold. Indeed a baboon, possessed by an evil spirit, is perhaps the nearest approximation one could find to the outward similitude of Mr. Tinctop's mamma.

"Beg your pardon, mother," Mr. Tinctop apologetically observed. "All grist that comes to the mill, I suppose. Go on with your story. Who else, besides the bishop's man and Sally from the square?"

"Wait a bit," his mamma responded, count-

ing the while on her skinny fingers, of which
the veins and arteries seemed all to have been
injected with purple sealing wax. There's
been a many more; but my poor old head
gets crazy and shaky-like now-a-days. There
was the Duchess of Minnever's maid, now."

Mr. Tinctop started in his chair, and turned
a yellow red—a sort of orange tawny in the
face, remarkably disagreeable to view.

" The Duchess of Minniver!" he exclaimed.
" What! has that white-faced cat returned to
England? I thought she was in Italy."

" She's in England, and in Belgrave Square,
sure enough," his mother resumed, nodding
her head; " Mrs. Cuppings—that's her maid's
name—was here at twelve o'clock, just arter
Mr. Premmuneer — that's his lordship the
bishop's gentleman—which I know him by
the token of being the nicest spoken gentleman as ever comed to a seckind-'and ward-
robe-shop, and always sending out for rum
and shrub to treat a body with like, quite
genteel; but do stick to his bargins, and
stand out for money, which have he will,
ascrewin' of you like an heathen Jew."

"Never mind the bishop's man, mother; I want to know all about my lady the Duchess." ("Burn my lady the Duchess!" he muttered to himself, between his clenched teeth.)

"Cuppins come with some fal-lals in a basket, which her missus give her on'y last night as bein' no good to her, and only fit to be worn among furrineers. There was a dozen pair o' lavender kid, six o' rose colour, four o' straw, three caffyolay — I think she called them—a bit of a rag of a lace scarf or two, a power o' silk stockins agone at the heel— she dances, so does the Duchess, Cuppins says—a real ingy shawl, but with a 'ole right through it, just as if it had been made with a red-hot poker; but Cuppins ses as how it was one of the Dook's cigars, as he is allers a smokin' of; a barridge dress over a pink slip, a black morry antick ——"

"Stop! stop!" interrupted the general practitioner. "I don't want to have the catalogue of the woman's wardrobe. I aint a broker's man. Tell me all about the jade herself.

The ladies' maid's tongue was sure to run nineteen to the dozen when the bargain was over."

" Mrs. Cuppins is a pleasant spoken body— oh! my bones, my blessed bones!"—the old woman moaned, rocking herself to and fro and feeling her joints. " She says the Dook's mortal fond of her."

" Of whom, Cuppins?"

" No: t'other, the Duchess. Spends a world of money on her. Ses she's the most beautiful creature of the day. So she is— Cuppins ses too."

" So is the Devil!" Tinctop broke in, in an irritated tone. " She's thirty-five, if she's a day."

" Cuppins says she aint thirty."

" Cuppins is a fool. Ten years ago she was twenty-five to my certain knowledge, though she didn't look more than eighteen, and that makes my calculation pretty correct. Go on with what the maid said about her."

" She's a carryin' on the same as usual," Mrs. Tinctop *mère*, proceeded. " Her 'ouse was full o' grand compinny, kings and markees, and captings, Rooshian Poles, and Boneyparties, when she was in them there foring parts; and now her 'ouse in London is as full. She do 'ave hall her sweets from Gunter's. She's got a French cook which speaks four languages, writes poetry and stuff, plays on the pianer, and sings comic songs beautiful. She's goin' to 'ave a grand ball to-morrow night, with eight ambassydors and Mr. Collinet's band."

" Anything else?"

" Ah! yes; well! There's lots of foring markees and captings hanging about the 'ouse, and makin' lov' to her, and a follerin' of her about like tame monkeys. The Dook gets wild at it sometimes, but he's so spooney on her he don't dare say nothin'."

" Go on."

" I don't know that I've got anything more to go on with. Oh, yes! There's a power of beggin' letter writers allers a plaguein' of her; and there's that painter feller, that crazy artist chap, that she's known ever so many years, has been hankerin' a'ter her, has been tryin' to get some money out of her."

"Painter feller! Artist chap! Ah! I know whom you mean. Philip Leslie; that's the name, isn't it?

"Philip Leslie! That's his name sure enough. Well, he'd called ever so many times while she was out of town; and no sooner was she back, but he must come again day after day, a wantin' to see her, notcomestanding she was always denied to him, which made him ferocious like a wagabone to the gentleman which opened the door, lettin' alone his worryin' the hall porter's life out. Well; she see him at last."

" Where ?" Mr. Tinctop asked eagerly.

" She was at the top of the stairs; he was in the hall, with a portfoley of drawings under his arm—precious ragged his clothes is—and she ordered him out. Told him that he was an ungrateful feller, and that she didn't want to have no more to do with him. Told Mr. Tiffiny, the hall-porter, to give him in charge to the pelisse if he come again. He cried, Cuppins ses, in the hall before all the servants. He told Tiffiny that the Duchess —when she was LADY BADDINGTON, you remember—had been the rooing of him. She had made him a murderer, he said. I wonder what he meant by that. What does he go about calling hisself a murderer for? He'll get hung some of these days. He told Cuppins which he met her at the airy gate, and talked to her through the palins', that he had a sick wife and child, and not a mossle o' bread to give 'em; and Cuppins, which is a tender-hearted girl—and more fool she to be so—give him a shillin'; but they saw him come out of the public-'ouse by the Mews half-an-hour afterwards, which it is supposed he drinks; and Mr. Tiffiny says he smelt o' rum hawful. And yet, by Mrs. Cuppins telling, the Duchess used to be kind enough to him. It was who but he with her till he married."

" He was a fool to marry," Mr. Tinctop said, softly; " he was a fool to marry, and have a sick wife and child. Poor devil! I remember him a fine-looking fellow enough, ten years ago, Philip Leslie."

" He's gray now," mumbled the hag.

Yes; gray now. Brother, your locks were brown ten years ago. When those ten promised years of mine are over, how many heads turned gray shall I meet with? And my own? Keep looking-glasses well from me—ten years hence.

" Have you anything more to tell me, mother ?" asked the general practitioner.

" Yes ! yes ! Just one bit of a thing more. Aha !"

She looked—her shrewd old head on one side again—the cunningest old woman that had ever lived since the days of Cumæan sibyl. She chuckled out " Aha !" again; and after much fumbling and groping in some mysterious and cavernous gap in her garments, which might, by an immense stretch of courtesy, be called a pocket, she produced a small quadrangular brown paper parcel, which she held in her shaking palm, regarding it with covetous eyes.

" Yes! yes!" she said. " Somebody else has been here! somebody that you've tried to see, and to find out for two years and a half gone and past, and that you've advertised in the noospapers and things for, and spent your beautiful money all to no purpose; somebody that you've told me of time after .time, and that you'd never have got a smell of, if it had not been for your poor old mother, which you laugh at and despise. Mrs. Lint's been here this arternoon, my son; and it was on arternoon's leave. She was bein' night-nurse at Saint Lazarus Horse-pital."

" Have your own way—talk as much as you like."

" And this isn't the fust time I've seen her neither. Four times has she been here this week, as you well know, for well I've told you; and each time have I pumped her, and probed her, and pricked her up; for she's dreadful old, and her memory's anigh gone. I'm old too," she remarked, parenthetically looking down at her dilapidated carcass;

"but oh! I'm sharp.　I'm sharp enough yet, Seth!"

" You're as sharp as a needle or a weazel, I know, mother," Mr. Tinctop interposed.

" You may well say that," Mrs. Tinctop observed, chuckling again with gratification at this well-timed compliment.　" I got the whole story out of her this afternoon.　How she was sent for by Mr Fleem, which is now a Barrownight, to nuss the sick woman on the wedding day.　How the poor ragged, drunkin thing told her that she was Mr. Falcon's own lawful wedded wife."

" She told me that too," Mr. Tinctop observed.

" How you sent her to sleep with some laudanum or stuff."

" I dare say I did; he, he!"

" But how she was too clever for you arter all.　For though the poor wretch, before you took her away, told you the whole story, thinking she was a going to die — which die soon afterwards she did; and told you too, besides, that Mr. Falcon, the grand gentleman

as killed hisself in a fit of apoplexy, was the
father of her child; that the child was a boy,
and that he had run away, but she thought he
was with a lot of circus riders at York, which
made you take most rampagious journeys all
over country, to every show, and every horse
rider's booth that could be seen, and all to
no purpose: though you was so precious
clever, she was a little too clever for you."

"How so?"

"I am tired, Seth; my poor old breath
won't hold out.   Give us a drop of comfort;
there's a dear?"

Mr. Tinctop poured from the candlestick-
blacking-bottle-spirit-flask a modicum of the
semi-transparent liquid into a broken egg-
cup with a club foot, which his parent tendered to him.   The harridan swallowed the
dram with a prolonged "Haho!" and a
smack of the lips of satisfaction; then further
refreshing herself with a pinch of snuff from
a screw of paper, which she carried apparently behind her left ear, she resumed her
discourse.

"When the poor creetur died," she said, "in that court in the Strand where you had persuaded her to come, thinking to cure her, and teach her to dance to your own tune: only she was marked for death, and out o' that house was never meant to come again, but feét foremost: Mr. Fleem he set about seeing her bein' berried decent and comfortable for the sake of the family. And so he has her berried quite genteel, instead of it's bein' a parish job; and gives his 'stifficate to say as how she'd died from nat'ral causes, which people allers does when they die and nobody expects 'em to; and as Mrs. Lint had been in the beginnin' of the bisness, and Mr. Fleem he wanted, bein' such great people, to keep things quiet, he employs Mrs. Lint to do all the layin' out, and everything quite nice and comfortable; on'y he gives her a precious blowin' up for goin' to sleep by the bed-side, tellin' her as how she'd sacrificed one, and pr'aps more than one, human life by it; but on'y excuses her 'cause she must have been drugged, ses he, by some scoundrel or other;

which it was you, my Seth, that give her
the sleepy stuff, which well I knows, 'avin'
told me; and like your mother's son it was,
on'y you was a bit awk'ard, and didn't
manage things quite closely enough. You
should have asked your mammy for a wrinkle
or two, my dear. Aha!"

She was quite garrulous and fluent by this
time, Mr. Tinctop's mamma. The "drop
of comfort" seemed to have given her new
strength. Her son bowed his head and
smiled grimly at the qualified compliment
she had vouchsafed to bestow on him. Then
she went on —

"She up and told Mr. Fleem the story
she had heard from the woman; but he
pooh-poohed her, good gentleman, and sed
the poor thing must have been ravin', and
gave her ten pounds to hold her tongue; and
between you and me, Mrs. Lint, which is
rather a muddle-headed woman, though a
well-meaning soul, couldn't make chalk nor
cheese, nor yet heads nor tails, out of the
story she'd heard; and did really think the

woman she had nussed was a wanderin' in her mind when she told her — she talked so wild and foolish like; and as Mrs Lint ses, ses she, it is n't onst nor twice, nor three times a week, I tell you truly mem, but a'most every night at the horsepital, as I hear the poor, feverish creeturs, with their broken harms and legs, and heads quite made into 'natomies with sticking-plaister; bein' beat with legs of tables by journeymen carpenters, which their husbands ought to be hung up by the heels for racketing of 'em so: it bein' all along o' the drink, which, get it onst into a man's head you can't get it out till violence he's done, and blood he will have, if it's transportation — though oftentimes there's faults on both sides, and the woman's the wust. And then, just when they're a wantin' the apple teas, and their sline draughts, they turn quite silly in their heads, and talk about being Popes of Rome and Hemperors of China, let alone Queen Victoria, and Lewis Phillips, and 'avin' millions of money in the bank which their

relations is a keepin' 'em out of; likewise
the throne of Spain, which if you were to
believe half such bamboozlin' nonsense you 'd
never have done."

"Do get on, mother," Mr. Tinctop said,
with a yawn, half of weariness, half of impatience.

"I am a gettin' on," his mamma answered,
sharply; "I must have my say, or else none
at all. Well, she laid her out, and took her
clothes as her perkysites."

"What has that to do with the matter?"

"You'll see. She brought the 'duds' here
to sell. They warn't worth much, sich rags,"
the old woman added, with ineffable disdain.
' I gave her a shillin', and quite enough too,
for the petticoats and things; but cur'ously
enough, she took a fancy to the creetur's
stays, and would n't part with 'em. Lord
knows why, for they were old and ragged
enough. She wore them stays for four
years, till they nearly fell off of her; then
pickin' of 'em to pieces to see if she could'nt
make a new pair out of 'em, she found this
little brown paper parcel, folded quite flat,

and sewed into the linin', and this parcel she sold me yesterday for twenty golden suvrins, which you give me to pay her; and little did she expect to get so much for it, havin' forgotten nigh all about the matter years ago, and scarce bein' able to read besides. And here's the parcel; and now I'm tired, Seth Tinctop, and mean to go to sleep a bit."

She handed him the packet, and sank back yawning, and groaning with fatigue into her chair.

He opened; turned over the enclosures, read, carefully refolded, put up the packet in his breast pocket, drew on his gloves, put on his hat and smiled.

" That will do," he said more softly than ever. " It is all here; everything I want. Now, Duchess of Minniver — Polly of Belgrave Square; now Falcons and Guys, and grandees, I have you all hard and fast. Marriage certificate — register of birth — certificate of baptism. All in that little packet. At last I have found an heir to the BADDINGTON PEERAGE."

CHAP. XLIV.

HER GRACE.

HIS GRACE THE DUKE OF MINNI-VER was a great prince in Israel. He stood six feet two in his stockings; he was freckled; he had a slight tendency to sore eyes, and his hair was of a hue so violently red, that it had almost a sound, and seemed to embody blind Professor Sanderson's idea of the colour of scarlet: "the sound of a trumpet." He was very well educated, even for a duke, and had written a bulky octavo volume on prevenient grace (he was of a theological turn of mind), which had been copiously reviewed in the Quarterlies, hebdomadally laughed at by "Punch," and which the cynics

and sceptics of the Enarcheonologos Club de-
clared to have been written by his Grace's
chaplain. He was immensely rich. Cuneiform
Castle and Babylas Park in England; Ramoth
Gilead House, all Minnivertown, and half the
Sesostris Mountains in Ireland; Glen MacCre-
mona, and immense pasture lands in the
Stradivarius burghs in Scotland; besides San-
dyshell Cottage, Undercliff, Isle of Wight;
the entire island of Buigna-Collah in the
Thulian Archipelago (a region producing
abundant crops of diminutive ponies, dwarf-
cows, and sea-kale, and in the caverns of whose
rocky headlands the well-known Ossian, sur-
named Macpherson, is supposed to have corrected his proof sheets, but whose inhabitants
had an unpleasant custom of dying of starvation
whenever the oat harvest ran short); and the
great Chateau de Fanfreluche in Dauphiné
(his Grace was Duke of Fanfreluche in
France, in right of his mother, the last heiress
to the great house of Frobichon-Fanfreluche—
see Braguedart and d'Hozier) with its huge
demesnes, its great vine land, and its impene-

trable forests, yet the lair, it was said, of the
wolf and the wild boar—these are as many of
his Grace's possessions as I can, on the spur of
the moment, call to mind. His solicitors, Messrs.
Huzz, Buzz, and Pildash, of Lincoln's-Inn-
Fields, knew a great deal more about them
than I do, and had a prodigious respect for his
Grace. So also had his bankers, Messrs. Scoop
and Coupon, of Lombard Street; his agent,
Lieut.-Colonel Blackship, R.N., in Ireland;
Mr. Duncan M'Sporan, Writer to the Signet,
his Grace's *homme d'affaires* in Edinburgh;
and his English land steward, Mr. Baglow,
who was a landed proprietor himself, and had
thoughts, men whispered, of going into Parliament some day for one of his Grace's
boroughs. His head-gardener was a fellow of
the Royal Society and a director of three railways. The sons of his tradesmen had commissions in the army, purchased for them by
their parents from the profits of the Duke of
Minniver's custom; and if it were possible
that a greater man in the world could be than
his Grace, it was certainly his Grace's valet-de-

chambre—I beg pardon, " my Lord Duke's
gentleman "—who had a coronet, worked in
the hair of a *coryphée* of her Majesty's Theatre,
in the corner of his pocket-handkerchief;
scented his whiskers with " Jockey Club "
perfume; belonged to a club (in Major Fou-
bert's passage, Regent Street,) where they
black-balled more members than the Travel-
lers', and had positively rejected the Russian
Ambassador's groom of the chambers, and her
Royal Highness the Duchess of Cambridge's
cook; wore an uncut diamond hanging to his
watch-chain, and went into the best society—
below the salt. The Duke of Minniver had
four livings in his gift, and the Bishop of
Bosfursus owed his mitre to him. Oxford
fellows and Cambridge wranglers believed in
him with intense reverence. He returned a
Member for Hoggum-cum-Homany (2 mem.,
pop. 9,302); he returned one for Ballyminniver,
County Clare, Ireland; he returned one for
the Stradivarius burghs, with so much ease,
and with such an utter absence of opposition,
that young Fitz-Dufferer, Lord Showful's son,

who was elected during a tour in the Holy
Land, was heard afterwards to say, that he
liked his seat very well, only he could never
find out in what part of Scotland the Stradivarius burghs were situated. Such, with lands
and beeves, rivers and lakes, woods and glens,
mountains and vales, deer forests and salmon
leaps, sheep walks and cattle pastures, castles
and palaces, was John Henry Tudor Mont-
morency Douglas Fanfreluche-Frobichon,
Fitzleman, Duke of Minniver, and a Peer of
the United Kingdom, Duke of Fanfreluche,
Marquis of Scratchallan, Earl of Mulcreasas,
Baron Foggo, a Baronet K.G., K.T., D.C.T.,
an Elder Brother of the Trinity House, Hereditary Grand Corn-cutter, a Trustee of the
British Museum, a Director of the Ancient
Concerts, Lord-Lieutenant of Vampshire, and
Colonel-Commandant of the Vampshire Yeo-
manry Cavalry, President of the Royal
Society of Lapidaries, Grand Master of the
Cagliostro Lodge of Freemasons, Chairman of
the Nor-nor-Eastern Railway, a Governor of
Christ's Hospital, Member of the Academies

of St. Vitus of Bergamo and St. Giles of
Bologna, and Seneschal of the Manoir of Fanfreluche.

This fortunáte man, then—a millionnaire,
high in the favour of his Sovereign, learned,
cultivated, a linguist, an artist, a writer on
prevenient grace, and a frequent lecturer at
the Hoggum-cum-Homany Literary and Scien-
tific Institution, and an occasional contributor
to first-class reviews and magazines, a patron
of innumerable philanthropic societies, an
orator on evangelical platforms, a chairman at
countless charity dinners, a *dilettante*, the
friend of the poor, the champion of his order,
the star of the peerage—had every advantage,
every gift, that can make life distinguished,
splendid, happy. His word was law. Miles
of English soil belonged to him. He had the
entrée of St. James's. Before the magnificence
of his titles and possessions German grand
dukedoms and Italian principalities, splendid
as they were, paled their ineffectual fires. He
was a greater prince than Schaumburg-Lippe,
than Hesse-Hombourg, than Turn and Taxis,

than Rüdesheimer-Marcobrunner. Had he
not a hundred and twenty thousand a year?
Huzz, Buzz, and Pildash were his bond-ser-
vants; Scoop and Coupon did him homage.
He was surrounded by lip-service and eye-
service, by vassals and dependents, by courtiers
and flatterers. He was, from the commencement, Porphyrogenitus, and his coronet cast a
purple shadow on him. As an infant in his
cradle—bald, toothless, naked, and helpless—
in the first hour of birth, he had more power
and influence, he commanded more reverence
and consideration, than all the wisdom and
learning and virtue of eighty years, in a common man, could secure. He ought to have
been the happiest man alive. He would perhaps
have enjoyed the maximum of human felicity,
if he had only been able to open his mouth in
the House of Lords, and if he had not been
eaten up with the king's evil.

Lazarus—Lazarus! ragged forlorn man,
whom Dives' footman repulses, whom the
porter of St. Stonyheart's Workhouse won't
admit into the receiving ward, it being after

hours, and who is perforce compelled to crouch under the lee of the workhouse wall all night —be thou not utterly cast down, Lazarus— without bread, without money, without shoes. The sun is yours, and the sky, and hope, and a better inheritance to come.   Envy not yonder countess in the carriage : she may have a cancer beneath that Malines lace.   Envy not Crœsus and his millions : he may be a bankrupt to-morrow, and a fraudulent one, and three months afterwards a felon in hodden gray, plaiting chair-bottoms in a whitewashed cell. Envy not the king in his crown : he cannot eat for fear of being poisoned, nor sleep for fear of being strangled.   Envy not this phantasm Duke of mine.   He had a hopeless impediment in his speech; and he was incurably scrofulous.

His Grace the Duke of Minniver was, at the commencement of the year 1842, a widower, being then himself in the thirty-seventh year of his age.   His married life had not been one of unmingled felicity.   Her Grace the first Duchess had been a Muscovite lady, the high-

born and beautiful Russian Princess Olga
Sardanapalasoff—daughter of the Emperor
Paul's Prince Gregory Sardanapalasoff, who
was such a favourite of that monarch, and
who afterwards assisted Counts Pahlen and
Zouboff in strangling him. To the world at
large she was a magnificent creature, with
lustrous eyes, with a dress all over diamonds,
an accomplished Houri, who spoke eight
languages, and sang like Madame Pasta. To
the Duke, *en petit comité*, she was an intolerable shrew, who bullied him, beat her children
unmercifully, swore in the French and Muscovite languages, and in bed had feet as cold
as icebergs. Her lady's-maids (she discharged
about one every fortnight) attributed to her
other vices, such as smoking cigarettes, playing
at cards and cheating thereat, and drinking
Eau-de-Cologne grog. It is certain, that she
led his Grace a terrible life; and that for the
last two years of her existence they did not
see much of one another. She died at Aix-
la-Chapelle, of a *maladie de langueur*, which is
an ailment invented by continental physicians,

and which may be a malady of anything. The "Morning Post," at home, was full of the record of her virtues, and spoke in feeling terms of the agonised bereavement experienced by her noble relatives; but from Aix-la-Chapelle to Hombourg they talked scandal of her in connection with the French Vicomte de Confiture-Poivres, and even poor little Baba Effendi, the *attaché* to the Turkish Legation at Munich. M. de Xhlaïbtchick, Russian Minister at the latter place, wrote home to his Government (*sous seing privé*) that "*cette diolesse*" was dead. They knew all about her in Count Orloff's private chancery, and in General Ignatieff's office. It is in this disrespectful manner that great people are talked about abroad after their death. We manage these things better in England. Nobody had a word to say, the other day, when Earl Fitzheavenborn died; and did'nt the Reverend Casyus Lacteal preach a funeral sermon over the Duchess of Castlefaggot, who was notoriously no better than she should have been, in which he said that her Grace had been a good Duchess upon earth, and that there was no doubt that in heaven she would occupy that distinguished position to which her rank and virtues entitled her.

His Grace of Minniver was not long incon-solable. He sought and wooed, not unsuccess-fully, the fascinating Dowager Viscountess Baddington, who was then turning the heads of half London—of all fashionable London, rather, which is perhaps the only London worth talking about — by her beauty, 'her accomplishments, and her wit. Lady Bad-dington had been a widow for nearly seven years. She had refused numberless offers. General Count Schaffskoff I., Ambassador of Austria, had asked her in marriage. The Right Reverend Charles James Dollyfus, just translated from the see of Brentford to the archiepiscopal throne of Mortlake, and sur-named "Jumping Jemmy," from his early addiction to the pleasures of the dance, had placed his crozier, his lawn sleeves, his shovel hat, and his rich revenues at her feet. Lord Chief Justice Suspercoll had intimated (in broad Scotch) his intention of making her his fourth wife. Captain O'Ho the Irish fortune-hunter, late of the auxiliary legion of her Majesty Isabella the Catholic, and a descendant of the O'Ho Gurroo spoken of in the annals of the Four Masters, had laid such violent siege to her—craving at first a reciprocation of his passion, and subsequently pecuniary assistance — that he had to be carried away from her door by the civil force; and the Viscountess's butler had to make a police case of it. At last came the Duke of Minniver; and, coming, he saw and conquered.

And so Généviève, Viscountess Baddington, became Duchess of Minniver.

When we last parted company with the widow of the peer who died in the doctor's shop, she was in the possession of a jointure of £20,000, the fairy mansion in Curzon Street, and a considerable amount of plate and jewellery. But Généviève of Baddington was a far more advantageous *partie* when she became the spouse of the Duke of Minniver.

In this wise: Charles Falcon, fifth Lord

Baddington, made a bad end of it in the winter of 1835; his viscera having been transfixed by a pistol-bullet one wintry morning after a Bal Masqué at the opera. He was slain (in perfectly fair fight) by a young Englishman named Leslie, with whom he had quarrelled on the previous night. By his death, the vice-comital title of Baddington became extinct; and, there being no other heirs in the male line, the estates and other entailed property reverted, according to the terms of the fourth Lord Baddington's will, to Généviève, his widow. She inherited, as her grandnephew had done so short a time before, little save a Gordian knot of embarrassments, broad acres ploughed up by post-obits, and rent rolls with leaden mortgages attached to them. Yet, strangely enough, as though Fortune were determined to favour this woman, as though the *Tempus edax rerum* were to be to her a revivifier, the ten years I have been harping on succeeded in changing most marvellously the complexion of the Baddington personalty. There were lands sold

under the Irish Encumbered Estates Act, and
the Dowager profited thereby; there were fat
leases that fell in, and were renewed on
payment of heavy fines; there were trunk-
railways and branch-railways driven through
the Baddington property by companies who
took up land peremptorily, whether they
wanted it or not, and paid for it exorbitantly,
to the glee of the land-holders and the dismay
and indignation (expressed by howls of
"shame" and " chair" at the quarterly meet-
ings) of the railway shareholders. Finally, a
sleepy old gentleman in a wig, with a large
quantity of snuff on his shirtfrill and his
cambric bands, and a rusty black gown hanging off rather than on his shoulders, delivered
himself one day in a back room in Lincoln's-
Inn-fields of a series of remarks quite inaudible
to three-fourths of his hearers, but which
occupied three hours and forty-four minutes in
their delivery. His auditory comprised some
horsehair sofa-cushions, several bags of crimson
moreen, a vast quantity of waste paper, tied
up with red tape, and scribbled all over with

nonsense in the English and Latin languages;
a madman or two, a deaf old woman or two,
an abstracted policeman, grown mildewed with
constant surveillance of the inns of court; an
usher with a red face, some clerks with white
ones, and a number of counsel more or less
learned in the law. His decision, whatever it
was, did not seem to create much excitement,
and the one short-hand writer present, gave
suspicious signs of somnolence during its
enunciation; but it leaked out from time to
time that he (the old gentleman in the wig)
would have liked to have had "more affi-
davits," and that the "costs must be costs in
the cause." Half an hour afterwards there were
little knots of men of legal mien chatting at the
portals of Serjeant's Inn, at the Burton ale
and sandwich shop at the corner of Cursitor
Street, and at the bar of the Mitre at the
Fleet Street end of Chancery Lane, where the
sheriff's officers wait for the habeas corpuses
to take their captives over to the Queen's
Prison—more familiarly known as the "Bench"
—where the law writers wait to see if there be

any manuscript at twopence per folio, or any eleemosynary drams of spirits to be had; and where those mysterious personages who were wont in the old time to perambulate the great saloon of the futile footsteps, Westminster Hall, with straws in their shoes, and whose occupation is not by any means gone now-a-days, are always in attendance in a philan-thropic eagerness to render service to suffering humanity—or, in other words, to become "bail" where bail is wanted, for a gratuity of from half-a-crown to twelve and sixpence. The barristers who alarm and astonish fo-reigners who meet them flying about Chancery Lane and the Rolls Yard, bewigged and in hybrid attire, had a great deal to say on the sleepy old gentleman's decision; and next morning the legal columns of the "Times" were filled with a report of the termination of the great case of "Falcon and Falcon" (both parties to which were dead and buried), where-with were connected the kindred suits of "Delahawk and another *versus* Falcon." "Falcon *versus* Rook," "Kitely's Charity,"

the " Attorney-General *versus* Redbreast," and
the " Churchwardens of Chaffincham-Regis
versus the Trustees of St. Vautour's Grammar
School." Nobody understood much about
these seemingly interminable cases, whose
intricacies had almost faded from the memory
of man, and the ink on whose parchment
records had grown rusty brown, like the blood
of a by-gone murder. The spiders must have
been sorry; the moths inconsolable; and I can
fancy a grim chorus of doleance in some misty
region of the legal shades of disembodied spirits
— ghosts of chaffwaxes, filacers, registrars,
prothonotaries, clerks of the pipe, assessors of
the petty bag, and tellers of the Exchequer—
groaning that Ichabod, his glory had departed,
and that the great Baddington Chancery suit
was at an end.

But Généviève of Baddington got — I hate
the inelegant Saxonism, but she "got" it,
strictly—ten thousand pounds a year. No
more, nor less. The Baddington estates were
hers. The Baddington heritage was hers,
principal and usufruct, income and mesne

profits; for, you see, there was no male heir to the peerage. Lord Baddington the fourth had not deemed his grand-nieces worthy of a thought, and the Lady Généviève had all.

Who showed herself, however, generous, almost to a fault, towards her impoverished connections by marriage; for relatives they could not be called. She first addressed most sisterly offers of assistance to Lady Guy, wife of Sir William Guy, Bart., of Mayford, Kent, who was leading a most ridiculously stupid and happy life, burying herself in the country, making flannel petticoats for old women, and having a large family of children. The grand-niece-in-law, however, who was a most singular young person, and had hitherto pertinaciously refused to hold any intercourse with Lord Baddington's widow, sent a frigid reply, to the effect that her husband's fortune was sufficiently ample, and that, thanking Lady Baddington, she declined her proposal. Nothing daunted, the Lady Généviève made amicable overtures to the widow of the late Gervase Falcon, Esq., of Grosvenor Square —

now very old, and poor, and paralytic. Her
daughters, now irremediable old maids — they
were young still, but Time uses poor people
so cruelly — had been entertaining serious
thoughts of trying their fortunes in Miss
Queechy Wetherell's " Wide, Wide World,"
as governesses, replied haughtily, that if the
Dowager Lady Baddington (they spoke of her
in their own circle as " that woman") chose
to render up any portion of the *patrimony of
their ancestors*, they would receive it as an act
of justice, but not of charity. To this com-
munication, which was written on paper with
a very black border (they had never gone out
of mourning for the young Lord killed in
Paris), their spiritual adviser, the Reverend
Brandley Burners, M.A., perpetual curate of
St. Tarbucket, added eight pages of alternate
exhortation and denunciation, abundant in
similes, and likening Lady Baddington, among
other unhandsome things, to Domdaniel, and
Eutychus that fell from the third loft. In a
postscript (p. 4) he dwelt upon the want experienced of a new rood-screen for St. Tar-

bucket's lady-chapel, and drew attention to the crying claims of the Associate Mission to the Web-footed Choctaws and the St. Tarbucket's Curates' Goloshes Mutual Aid Society. Lady Baddington laughed, and settled an income of three hundred and fifty pounds a-year upon Mrs. Falcon's daughters. The settlement was effected through her solicitors, Messrs. Huzz, Buzz, and Pildash; and the Misses Falcon improved the first opportunity of meeting her in the street, prior to their permanent *avatar* to Tours in France, to cut Lady Baddington dead in the Soho Bazaar.

So Généviève, whom Mr. Tinctop called Polly, was rich thricefold, and was Duchess of Minniver. And so there be some of us who ride upon white elephants, and have bangles of gold and jewels on our arms; and some that wear hemp on the neck and gyves on the ankles, and are handled by the hangman.

CHAP. XLV.

THE DUCHESS OF MINNIVER RECEIVES A DISTINGUISHED CIRCLE.

THE Lady Généviève's entertainments were the strawberry leaves and cream of fashionable life. Almacks was not more exclusive. Indeed, many considered it to be much easier to procure a voucher granting admission to those skyblue saloons with the cracked walls, than to secure a card for one of the Duchess of Minniver's ineffable entertainments. The great author of "Vanity Fair" once favoured his readers with what he doubtless considered to be an infallible recipe for getting into good society. "If you wanted to be asked to dinner," he says, "*ask to be asked.*" I think the Duchess of Minniver would have

taken a vast amount of asking before she had
condescended to ask any one to her board
whom it was not her gracious pleasure to
receive.

The London season had had its triumphs,
and was now in the wane. Her Majesty's
Theatre — people had not heard of Mr. Gye
then — was closed. Grisi and Mario were off
to the Continent to earn a few hundred
thousand francs before wintering in St. Petersburg. The men in the red jackets began to
disappear from St. James's Street and Pall
Mall; the fogies began to reign undisturbed
in the bow-windows of the clubs. There
were fewer amazons in Rotten Row — fewer
broughams, with lapdogs looking out of the
windows, in the Ladies' Mile. The courteous
shopmen at the circulating libraries were no
longer overwhelmed with demands for the last
new novel (no circulating library will ever be
overwhelmed with demands for this); hothouse pines no longer absorbed the attention
of Mr. Staymaker, of the Grand Avenue,
Covent Garden Market; Mrs. Buck, over

against St. Paul's Church, ceased in her hitherto ceaseless occupation of making up bouquets for fashionable soirées; the affable Mr. Shee, at Cramer and Beale's, was pestered no more for Linley's ballads or Thalberg's variations; Swan and Edgar, and Howell and James's, journeymen had breathing time; Mr. Hancock, the jeweller, began to post up his diary of conversations with the crowned heads of Europe during the past three months; the lodging-house keepers of Brighton and St. Leonards began to rub their hands. Among the continental hotel-keepers, from the brigands of Boulogne to the vampires of Venice, there arose a shout of gratulation at the thought of the approaching rush of autumnal tourists; Mr. Albert Smith (had he invented Mont Blanc then, which he hadn't) would have been rushing in a Hansom to some railway terminus whose line had the most branches, devising, as he sped, some new way of reaching the monarch of mountains — this time, perchance *viâ* the caves of Elephanta, Honolulu, and Lake Tschudi. The House of

Commons was massacring new-born bills with Herodian cruelty and celerity; the Ministerial whitebait shuddered, in their tanks off Greenwich, at the thought of their coming martyrdom by batter and bedevilment; theatrical managers took tickets for Paris, to see what was going on at the Palais Royal, or the Porte St. Martin; and the LONDON SEASON was doomed.

But Géneviève, Duchess of Minniver, was determined to be in at its death; and she issued cards for a grand *soirée dansante*, to be holden at her mansion in Belgravia — Parliament sate late that year — in the last half of the month of August. The invitation kept many noble families in town: they could not miss the dear Duchess's ball, they said; and the Misses Falcon at Boulogne coming from M. Adam's, the banker's, where they had been drawing their quarterly stipend, and sailing into the reading-room in the Rue de l'Ecu to read "Galignani," wondered how that designing creature had ever managed to get into society. "If it hadn't been for our poor dear uncle's infatuation," they said——

Their poor dear grand-aunt was going to Grand Cairo, Jerusalem, the white Nile, *que sais-je?* at the end of the season, and she was determined her last ball should be a grand one. She took the House of Lords and the House of Commons and shook them carefully in a sieve, separating the wheat from the chaff; she filtered the *corps diplomatique*, retaining the most pellucid drops thereof; she distilled the "Court Guide" in an alembic of much power; fumigated "Webster's Royal Red Book;" visited the fashionable menageries, and took the lions that roared the loudest; skimmed off the *crême de la crême* of rank, beauty, and fashion, extracted a few flasks of attar from some bushels of aristocratic rose-leaves — and issued her cards of invitation accordingly.

There was wailing and gnashing of teeth, or simperings of pleasure, or croakings of envy, or titterings of suppressed mortification, as her powdered footmen — she had so many now that she could scarcely count them — bore round her perfumed missives, with the ducal coronet on the seal. To be asked to the

Duchess of Minniver's was like being asked to one of Louis Quatorze's hydraulico-pyrotechnic *fêtes*. It was *être de Marly*, as it is *être de Compiègne* now-a-days. So eager were people to come to her feasts, that she had but one answer declining her invitation. It was from old Lady Golgother (Lady Golgother of the Regency, and before the Regency; of before the Flood, the backbiters whispered), who was ninety, and died the week afterwards, and could therefore, I think, be rationally excused. The fashionable milliners had a hard time of it to make the dresses that were required for the festivity; but they consoled their over-tasked workwomen by telling them that this was to be the last ball of the season. Sir Townsend Towser, of the Life Guards, who was labouring under a temporary difficulty in the Valley of the Shadow of Debt — to the extent, indeed, of inhabiting apartment No. 9 in 2 in the Queen's Bench — regretted his incarceration deeply. Had he been free, or rather not supposed to be travelling in Italy, he told Lumpey of the Blues and Clumpy of

nothing particular save the clubs, he would
have been sure to have received an invitation
for the Duchess's ball; in which assurance —
the Duchess knew perfectly well where he
was — Sir Townsend Towser was grievously
mistaken.

Sir Paracelsus Fleem was invited. Yes. He
went everywhere; though he confessed himself,
sometimes quite pleasantly, that his father sold
coal and potatoes, not in a shop, but in a shed.
He went everywhere, from the Queen's Palace
to the most miserable den in the lowest
lodging-house in St. Giles's. He was asked
everywhere, and had everybody's ear, though
he was not a great talker; but, curiously to
say it, whenever anybody talked to Sir
Paracelsus Fleem, they told him the truth.
For it is no good lying to a doctor, my friend;
if you do, you die.

And Mr. Seth Tinctop, M.R.C.S., was he
invited? No. He was not, you know, "in
society"·—that is, in the creamy, ineffable,
Grand Laman Society, which alone could
satisfy the Minniver exigencies. Yet he was

not by any means the same humble Mr. Tinctop we knew ten years since, keeping the
doctor's shop in Drury Lane. The beneficent
years had done him good too, as it seemed.
He felt the pulses of titled people now, and
attended earls' children through the measles.
But it was always in a sort of secondary
capacity. He always attended in lieu of
somebody else, or was providentially in attendance to supply the place of somebody,
or in somebody's unavoidable absence was
kind enough to do what was required; but
it was always understood, or he made it
understood, that he was not the genuine
article, but a substitute, a kind of albata
or Sheffield plate, very serviceable and useful,
but not the real thing. Don't you know
such people, who throughout their lives,
sometimes involuntarily, but as frequently
of their own free will, are first lieutenants,
chief clerks, grand viziers, foremen, and stage
managers, but never become captains, mer-
chants, sultans, masters, or lessees? They
are marked B 2 for life, and seem to like

it. Mr. Tinctop had a carriage now, a diminutive one-horse carriage, and a footman with
one black epaulette. He gave quiet little
bachelor dinners, where there was French
cookery and good wine. A man of cosmo-
politan tastes, Tinctop, he could relish his
pipe and his whiskey-and-water elsewhere;
and he dwelt — wherever do you think? —
in the fairy mansion in Curzon Street, which
he rented of the Duchess of Minniver's land-
agents. But it was a fairy mansion no more.
The door was half covered by a big brass
plate, highly polished; there was a night
bell; and within the fairy furniture was
replaced by steady, medical-looking goods and
chattels. Double door to dining-room; inner
one communicating with study of green baize
with brass nails. Sarcophagus wine-cooler.
Portraits of Sir Astley Cooper and Sir Paracelsus Fleem. Bust of Galen. Bust of
Grecian female, name unknown, with a
straight nose and a round chin. (Why
should medical men always have that un-
named female's bust in their houses? Is

she the Goddess Hygeia, I wonder?) Round table in the waiting-room, with Boyle's "Court Guide," the "Medical Directory," and an odd . volume of "Thaddeus of Warsaw," to amuse the patients. Everything decorous, medical, strictly in accordance with medical propriety. Oh! he was a wary man!

Mr. Tinctop was not asked to the Duchess of Minniver's ball, although he was one of her medical attendants in ordinary. Her Grace would have just as soon perhaps invited her grocer or her cheesemonger; yet the non-arrival of an invitation did not hinder Mr. Tinctop from driving to the Duchess's mansion in Belgrave Square — Minniver House, in Piccadilly, that great jail-like palace with the brick wall in front, *edificatum temp. Georg. III.*, was under repair just then, and they had taken the house in Belgravia for two years — did not hinder him dismissing his carriage, nodding familiarly to the footman, and walking straight up-stairs to the Duchess's dressing-room. In truth, he was as free of the house as a cat; and the

Duke, when he met him on the staircase and encountered his sly salutation, was rather afraid of him than otherwise.

It was ten o'clock at night, and the house was a blaze of light. There were wax candles in girandoles everywhere, shouldering the gas, as though they considered that outspoken element to be a low vulgar fellow, fit only to flare in butchers' shops, and not half expensive enough. On the grand staircase there were rows of exotic plants in boxes; the saloons were full of vases of odoriferous flowers. Gunter's men were pouring down the area steps. The groom of the chambers — she had a groom of the chambers! — was disciplining his larynx with Doctor Stolberg's voice lozenges, preparatory to his arduous task in announcing the company. The link-boys were aware of the great merrymaking, and came trooping down, their chief with a silver badge on his ragged jacket, hugging themselves in the anticipation of half crowns. Picked men of the A division of police condescended to partake in the (out-door) solemnities. The housekeeper was in the still-room the butler in the pantry; the reporter for the "Morning Post" — a languid gentleman in whiskers — was sipping chambertin in a private apartment, placidly contemplating the cream-laid and gilt-edged paper, the crow-quill pens, and the violet ink (scented), with which the Duchess's secretaries imagined he would indite his lucubrations. The groom of the chambers and his Grace's gentleman, M. Jabot made much of Mr. Penguin of the "Morning Post." Mr. Shantilly, who was there from Messrs. Gunter's to supervise, made much of him; Mr. Sphoon, the butler, contemplated him with reverential awe, as a man "who wrote in the noosepapers;" the Duchess had sent down word that he was to be treated with every consideration. The lady's maid was captivated with his whiskers, and envied his languidness. Mr. Penguin, who was a philosopher of the school of Democritus, who knew the aristocracy better than Garter King-at-Arms, and nearly as well as a bill discounter, who exchanged nods with marquises, and was on pinch of snufftaking terms with the *corps diplomatique*, took all this homage in very good part. He might have had his brougham filled — Mr. Penguin kept a brougham — with cases of champagne, trifles, ice-creams, gooseberry fool, pot and hothouse flowers, if he liked. Lords made quite as much of him as their retainers. Prime Ministers clapped him on the shoulder, and told him to make as much as he could of that little speech at the wedding-breakfast. Dowager Countesses were anxious to know if he had been made quite comfortable, and if he had heard quite distinctly Lord B.'s *beautiful* remarks on conjugal love. He looked much more like a Lord than three-fifths of the Peerage, and had more than once been mistaken for one by the door-keepers of the House of Peers. Mr. Penguin did not write his report on the cream-laid paper, or with the crowquill pens. He wrote it instead on little shabby slips of flimsy paper, which he delivered to a little ragged boy with a gummy face, *semi*-sable, who was sleeping under a bench at the public-house round the corner in the Mews. Then Mr. Penguin, with an opera poncho thrown over his evening dress, but with his white neck-cloth still very resplendent, would walk down to the " Crimson Hippopotamus " in the Strand — that famous night-house of call for morning newspaper men, and have a Welsh-rabbit and a glass of hot gin and water for his supper. He was always affable —never proud, never supercilious, though he lived among the *kaloi kai agapoi*. As Mr. Tinctop passed upstairs, he became aware of the arrival of Mr. Collinet's band, who were tuning their instruments, and causing them to emit rueful remonstrances of sound, in the grand saloon, where the dancing was to take place. There was to be a concert before the ball, too; and Signor Francisco Pulcinella, from Bergamo, the accompanyist, was torturing a grand pianoforte to the proper concert pitch. Mr. Tinctop winced somewhat at the discordant sounds, then grinned that own peculiar grin of his, and pursued his way upwards.

The Duchess's dressing-room — he knew it full well — lay at the extremity of a long suite of sumptuous apartments now darkened and devious. But Mr. Tinctop threaded them all, and arrived at last at the entrance to the sacred *boudoir*, whose portals were shrouded by white curtains in cut velvet of Utrecht.

He paused ere he entered, though his hand was on the drapery, and with an inexpressibly cunning face, listened. He heard a sound as of some one weeping, and in dire distress.

Had he entered, he would have found, kneeling on the ground, with her head buried in the cushion of a great carved and gilded *fauteuil*, a beautiful woman half dressed, with her golden hair floating over her bare shoulders, and sobbing, and murmuring, and writhing, and twining her slender fingers, one within the other, as though she would have broken them.

CHAP. XLVI.

MR. TINCTOP SPEAKS HIS MIND.

THE sound of a woman weeping is not ordinarily one of pleasure to manly ears.
" Beauty disarmed," " Beauty in tears,"
" Beauty in distress:" these are refrains to
the old nautical or sentimental ditties our
grandmothers used to sing to the spinet and
the harpsichords, in the unsophisticated days
when it was not thought that good music was
spoilt by having good words set to it. Such
words awakened enthusiasm, or, at least, sympathy. *Planco consule;* but Mr. Tinctop did
not recognise Plancus or his consulate, and
sympathy and enthusiasm were drugs not to
be found in his pharmacopœia. To all the

sobbings of Beauty in distress within — for he
knew well enough whose voice it was he heard
—he replied only by a shrug of the shoulders,
a shrewd suppression, and then an interroga-
tive protrusion of the lips, and by waiting.
Beauty, on the other side of the door, grew
more tranquil anon; and then Mr. Tinctop
turned the handle of the lock, and went into
the chamber.

The Frenchwoman, her maid (Cuppins was
not *de service* that evening)—an ill-looking
handmaiden enough, with two black lustrous
bandeaux of hair on her temples, eyes that
sparkled like jet beads, and a face so yellow
and wrinkled as to present an unpleasant resemblance to the physiognomy of a toad, that
had been taking a nap in the centre of a
block of marble for a century or two — came
running towards Mr. Tinctop as he entered,
putting forth her meagre hand as though to
stay him, and crying, that "*Madame la Du-
chesse était en déshabille.*" But the medical
practitioner continued imperturbably to advance; and the Duchess of Minniver, rising

from her chair, bade him come in and her maid leave the room at one and the same time. The Frenchwoman (Mademoiselle Ame-naide, I think, was her name, but as you will meet her no more in this history, it does not much matter) shrugged her lean shoulders, paused to envelop her mistress in a loose peignoir of white China silk and disappeared. Mr. Tinctop very gravely walked up to the dressing-table; sat down in the carved and gilded fauteuil, on whose cushions the fevered cheeks of the Duchess of Minniver had rested a few moments before; and took as calm and equable a survey of the apartment and its occupant, as though he had been a member of the Society of Antiquaries in an inedited cathedral crypt, or a detective policeman in a room where a murder or a burglary had just been committed, or a broker's man in a household where there was something worth seizing.

He nodded his head softly as he looked, as though he approved highly of the internal arrangements of her Grace the Duchess of

Minniver's dressing-room.   And, in truth, it
was a goodly sight, making the fairy palace in
Curzon Street quite mean and shabby by
comparison.   Silk and gilding, lace and velvet, rare woods, wax candles, crystal lustres,
lace fringes and tassels.   The dressing-table
was an altar.   The vast mirror was a marvel
of silver and mother-of-pearl, and was held up
by alabaster Cupids shrouded in Brussels lace.
The *nécessaire de toilette* was a casket of
treasures.   There were jewelled nail-scissors,
bodkin cases of malachite and gold, hair-
brushes with backs of silver filagree.   The
stoppers of the perfume bottles glistened and
sparkled in the candle light.   The lip-salve
was in the bosom of a little golden hawk,
chased and enamelled, with emerald claws and
ruby eyes. Strewn all about were the plumes,
the gauzes, the flounces, the braveries and
fripperies which the beautiful woman was to
wear that night.   Flaming like fire were the
superb jewels in their morocco cases.   Blatant
everywhere, on jewel-case and toilet linen, on
the stoppers of flasks and the escocheons of

toilet boxes, were the two ducal coronets; one with strawberry leaves, for England, one with spikes and fleur-de-lis erased, for France; and the two ciphers, M. and F., for Minniver and Fanfreluche.

The Duchess stood up, just opposite Tinctop, looking at him. She had folded her arms over her beautiful shoulders, which rose and fell with the heaving of her bosom. Her little feet beat the devil's tattoo impatiently on the velvet-piled carpet. Her cheek was flushed, her eye flashed. She was a thousand times more beautiful than any of the jewelled gewgaws, the luxurious toys in that room; but Tinctop scarcely looked at her. At last the little silver hammer of an alabaster clock on the mantel began to set its bell a-tingling; whereupon she spoke.

" What do you want here, bird of ill omen?" she asked, with an assumption of cheerfulness, but her voice trembling oddly as she spoke. " Tiresome creature; you always come when I am dressing. If you were not my *médecin intime* my husband would be jealous."

" Your husband!"

" The Duke of Minniver," she retorted,
turning deadly pale, and then as violently
red. " What do you want, tyrant, persecutor,
despot? Money? What do you want with it
all; with your one-horse brougham, your dingy
furniture, and your white neckcloth? You
must be as rich as a Jew, or must gamble, or
else you must spend your money upon opera
dancers. Tell me, Seth — now there's a dear
—what you want to-night? It's getting late,
and I must be dressed and down stairs by
eleven. I haven't been home half an hour
from the Palace."

She had been dining with her Sovereign
that very evening. The Duke of Minniver
was, as you already know, Hereditary Grand
Corncutter, an office conferred upon the first
Duke, Robert Fitzleman, by his royal master,
Charles the Second, of philoprogenitive memory, and for discharging the onerous duties
of which office he drew an annual salary of
two thousand pounds from an undertaxed
country. By the way, the first Fitzleman

might, with a little more propriety perhaps, have been called Fitztrollop; for his mamma, according to the *chronique scandaleuse* of the Restoration, was in the habit of dancing corantos on a cord distended across two poles, at Bartholomew Fair. His sacred Majesty, they say—but no, there must be no scandal against Queen Elizabeth or King Charles the Second, at this time of day. At any rate, the first Fitzleman was uncommonly like his papa in feature, when he wore a perriwig; and it was his good fortune to live in those halcyon days, when the sons of tight-rope dancers not unfrequently became dukes.

She had been dining with her Sovereign, where she had fed off gold, had only spoken when she was spoken to, and had come away rather hungrier than she went. Eating at dinner was not then considered fashionable at Court. The Duke, as Hereditary Grand Corn-cutter, had been spoken to twice by H.R.H. the Prince Consort; during the rest of the repast, the Duke of Minniver crumbled his bread, and looked at himself in his golden spoon. One of the maids of honour had giggled during the *entrées*, and told her neighbour —. an Archbishop — that the Duke of Minniver used too much Macassar oil to make his hair look brown. The Archbishop—our old friend " Jumping Jemmy "—suggested hair-dye, and chuckled, whereupon Royalty had frowned sternly on the pair; in consequence of which, I presume the maid of honour was sent to the Tower that very night, after having been summarily corrected, in nursery fashion, by the Court duenna or Mother of the maids, and the Archbishop relegated to his see, there to translate his Latin Pastorals into Greek Iambics, till he showed signs of better behaviour.   I know the discipline at Court is very strict.   There had been a Royal Duke present at the dinner, who remarked to the Great Captain of the Age (who was dining on a French roll) that the *vol-au-vent à la financière* was " very good, very good, very good," three times.   There was a prodigious old Guy of a German princess, done up in crimson satin, who gobbled over her food, and expectorated freely in Mechlin lace: and this is, I declare, an accurate description of the dinner at Buckingham Palace, from which Généviève, Duchess of Minniver, had just come. I am not drawing from imagination. I had the picture from a Royal footman, who turned author and died.

She had driven straight away from the royal table (being excused in consequence of her entertainment), but was too proud and beautiful to wear her dinner-dress.

"What do you want?" she asked again, impatiently, almost harshly, for Mr. Tinctop had never answered a word yet.

He rose, and leaned his back against the glittering dressing-table. He took up one of the morocco dressing-cases, and with his fore-finger—it was an ugly forefinger, with a nail which, mown, pared, scraped as it was, looked like a claw—struck the coronets and the initials stamped in gold upon the leather. Struck them violently—struck them scorn-fully.

"Do you see this, you jade?" he said, at last.

" Yes;" she answered, trembling.

" You a duchess — you the widow of a viscount — you the heiress of all the Baddington estates — you the leader of rank and fashion—you the Queen of Beauty! I'll queen of beauty you, you gipsy!"

" What have I done?" she faltered.

" Done! What haven't you done? Aren't you mine, body and soul? Aren't you my goods and chattels, my property, my household stuff?   Did I pick you up out of the mud, out of the gutter, when you were dancing in frilled trousers and spangles, with a monkey, a white mouse, and a Savoyard organ-grinder, in the streets of Genoa?"

She started at him in dumb horror, but pointed to the door.

" Nobody's listening; and if anybody should be, I do not care," Mr. Tinctop went on.   He was not, it must be admitted, with all the violence of his language, speaking beyond his usually calm, equable tone of voice.   " I'm going to speak my mind to you, my lady; and you shall hear it."

"You are speaking it strangely, Seth Tinctop."

"Exactly as I intend to do, *Mrs. Tinctop.* You were Lady Baddington, were you? You let me buy your dainty body from the Italian showman, who had bought you from the English mountebank, who had picked you up at an Irish fair, strumming a tambourine in front of a booth, and belonging to a gang of gipsies, or thieves, or worse. You let me receive your fine ladyship from your play-fellows—the monkey and the organ-grinder, and the cudgel of Giovanni your master. You let me put you to school; half ruin myself, to cram accomplishments into that clever, impish head of yours. You let me, before the English Consul at Turin, make you MY WIFE——"

"For God's sake stop, you madman," the woman cried out, springing across the room, and placing her hand on her self-styled husband's mouth. "Do you want us all to be ruined?"

"I want some one to be ruined, and I won't

stop," rejoined the implacable Mr. Tinctop, disengaging his mouth, with a gesture which looked very much as though he wished to bite the hand before him. " Didn't I marry you, Polly Draggletail, which is about all the name you have; my Lady Généviève, Duchess of Minniver, and all the rest of it, as you call yourself."

She looked at him with inexpressible loathing, hatred, contempt; but she did not spring upon him to rend him; she did not strike him with her strong white arm; she did not even spit upon him. She was cowed and beaten, and pressed her fingers on her throat as though she was choking; then replied—

" You did?" very slowly and subdued.

"And," Mr. Tinctop continued, speaking more rapidly, but not rising a quarter of a note in his vocalisation, "didn't you run away from me a month after marriage, when I had been fool enough to fall in love with you, and to spend, in dresses and trinkets for your worthless body, nearly all I had left of the money I had got from old Lord Baddington?

Didn't you go vagabondising about the country with swindlers, and horse jockeys, and cardsharpers, and half-pay captains, and German barons, and Italian counts, growing more beautiful, and more wicked, and more cunning every day, till you hooked the superannuated old fool Baddington, and decoyed him into marrying you? Marry, ecod! a nice wedded wife you were."

He had not libelled her—Tinctop. This, then, had been her career. It was hard to think of her, with her white neck and golden hair—so beautiful, so pure, so virginal —all widow as she was: it was very hard to think of her, depraved, corrupted, abandoned —a vicious, hardened wanton. Could a soul so blackened dwell in so fair a frame?

" When you went away—ran away—Polly, Jenny, Généviève, and so forth—ran away and left me almost beggared, and three-parts distracted at losing you—I swore that sooner or later I *would be revenged upon you.* I'm a quiet man, my dear, as you know full well. I'm not much given to romantic ideas, or that sort of nonsense; but if I don't bark I bite sometimes rather sharply; and I think, when I swear to be revenged upon anybody, I can take a leaf out of the book of those old Borgias, and the people who used to give the Aqua Tofana, and that sort of stuff."

" What do you want?" she murmured, more mechanically, it seemed, than with any distinct apprehension of the meaning of her words.

" You'll pretty soon know what I want," he answered coldly; " and I won't take many words to tell you in; for you must finish dressing, my angelical partner, and receive your grand company. It isn't money, however, I want; I've got lots of my own. I could get lots more from you. I could draw thousands from the red-headed dolt who thinks himself your husband — draw them from him by crooking my little finger. He would do anything I ask him, the Duke, for the honour of the house of Minniver-Fanfreluche is something; and I want to ruin the house of Minniver-Fanfreluche, Polly, my dear. I want to drag the coronet and the strawberry leaves all down into the mud, and the Duke and the Duchess with them. Aha!"

He spoke out loud *for the first time*—this ordinarily placid Tinctop. He said "Aha!" almost in a shriek. He was elated, triumphant; but she flinched no more, and looked at him with eyes of fire, daring him.

" Do your worst. How can you prove it? No one will believe your story. The Consul went mad and died. I don't believe it was a marriage at all. I had the certificate. You left it with me, and I burnt it."

She fired off these dislocated members of a phrase, and then began to pant. She was exhausted; she was tired.

" A fig for the Consul; a fig for anybody believing me or my story. I'll prove it fast enough when the time comes. I've another story to prove first. I have to prove the existence—and to prove it I've certificates that you haven't burnt, my lady—of the rightful heir to that Baddington peerage which you and many other fools thought extinct. I have that to prove that the young lordling who was killed in Paris was a bastard, and that the eldest son of Gervase Falcon, and the rightful heir to the peerage, is alive."

" Who is he; where is he?" she whispered hoarsely.

" Who is he?   Where is he?   I'll find him safe enough.   Wire by wire, and link by link, I've got this chain of evidence together.   I tell you I have found him. I tell you that I'll spend thousands to establish his claim before the House of Lords, to rout you out of the possession of his estates.   Then when I have made him a lord, and brought his half sisters to shame, I'll turn to you again my lady, and pull *your* pride down.   You a duchess — you a viscount's widow!   I'll prove to all the world that you're no better than the commonest wench that walks the streets.   I will, by —— !"

Why had she not a pistol now to shoot him as he spoke?   She used to have pistols.   Why had she not some subtle poison in her toilet case that she might cast over him, and burn his wicked tongue out? But she could do nothing but clasp her throat again, and in stifled accents ejaculate—" Mercy—mercy!"

" Mercy! I'll see you hanged—I'll see you burned in brimstone—first! I've given you plenty of law, Mrs. Polly; but now I mean to have my innings. There's only one more thing I have to tell you. Wouldn't you like to know who the new Lord Baddington is? I'll tell you. I'm sure you'll be glad to hear it. He's an old friend of yours. He's the poor devil of a painter whom you took up in one of your high and mighty caprices, and then cast away like a broken fan. He's the miserable, half-starved wretch with the sick wife and child, whom you had turned out of your house by your servants. He's Philip Leslie."

She might have been Lazarus, standing up in his grave in his cerecloth, she looked so ghastly, before the glittering toilet table standing in her china-silk *peignoir*. She did not scream; she could not scream; but with a low moan fell on the floor and fainted.

When her maid, hearing the fall, rushed in from the adjoining bed-room, and raised her mistress, she found that Mr. Tinctop had taken his departure. She thought it odd, as she applied the usual restoratives. *Ce n'était rien qu'une attaque de nerfs*, Mademoiselle Amenaïde told her Grace, when she recovered.

Mr. Tinctop walked very softly down the grand staircase, paying especial attention to the exotic plants which lined them, and apparently thinking them very pretty. He remarked to the hall porter who opened the door for him, that it was a beautiful night, but rather close.

The Duchess of Minniver's closing ball was the greatest triumph that London season had witnessed. The *Morning Post* had three columns of report next day; and his Grace the Duke had serious thoughts in his red head of asking the Prime Minister whether he could not make Mr. Penguin something under Government. The unconscious Penguin (who, to his honour be it spoken, would have indignantly refused the Goverment appointment, had it been offered to him) was, by the time his Grace had begun to speak about him, scouring the London and North-Western Railway on a special engine, in quest of the earliest information relative to an old woman of eighty-five, who had murdered her granddaughter with a reaping-hook.

Her Grace the Duchess was charming. Never had she been seen so beautiful, so full of spirits, of wit, and repartee. Everybody was enchanted; and dancing was kept up till five o'clock in the morning. Then Géneviève Duchess of Minniver went to bed.

To bed, but not to sleep. To think.

"It must be done," she murmured, for the twentieth time, tossing her burning head on her pillow. "Pollyblank! Pollyblank! yes, that was the wretch's name!"

His Grace the Duke had his own apartments in a separate part of the house. I wonder, had he heard his wife murmur that strange name, if any thoughts would have come across his mind akin to those that troubled Parisina's lord?

CHAP. XLVII.

THE ELEVENTH HOUR.

THE last grand entertainment of the fashionable season being over, and the season
itself having thus come to a legitimate and satis-
factory termination, the clerk of the weather determined, to all appearances, to be also in the
fashion, made up his meteorological mind to
give the Londoners no more fine weather, and
was, accordingly, " down on them " with a first
of September of the bitterest autumnal description. Mr. Kenny Meadows, that delightful artist, was then at home drawing beautiful
vignettes of " Autumn " on wood, for the illus-
trated newspapers. He represented the season
as a blooming brunette, luxuriously reclining

among luscious fruits, in a bower overshadowed by pulpy vines. Artists were out on their autumnal-sketching tour, running races with the mist up Saddleback or Helvellyn, or washing in their bits of rock and foliage in the inn-parlour of Betty's-y-Coyd; the smiling Welch landlady looking on approvingly as she fried her eggs and bacon; Jack Harold, the man who paints sunsets so well, singing that famous song of his about the three bank directors who went "fishing for roach and dace;" and Baronial Hall Springfield, with his tremendous red beard, arguing on German art with Waterfall Talmash and Bill Rokes, surnamed the "indefatigable," because he came to Wales every year for artistic purposes, and never painted anything but the portrait of the landlady's last baby. Men put uncharitable constructions even on this solitary pictorial annual; and said that Bill painted the portrait *for reasons* — for causes, in fact, connected with his weekly account current for board and lodging. It was the first of September, and they were gathering in the hops in Kent, and the apples in

Devonshire, and the corn everywhere, save only
in the bleak uplands of Scotland, where they
waited for October even to sharpen the sickle.
Foolish men took out game certificates; put on
absurd costumes; tramped over stubble fields,
bought birds of suburban game-dealers; and,
coming home to their wives or clubs, said they
had shot partridges. The grouse were uncommonly strong on the wing on the Scottish
moors; and no less stronger on the wing were
the insolvents of fashion, who flew right away
to Antwerp and Boulogne, defying the long
shots of their vengeful creditors, and laughing
merrily at the facetious proclamations of out-
lawry made once a month by Mr. Hemp, in
the Sheriff's Court. It was still hot and
sultry in Paris; the back streets smelt very
strongly of melons and peaches; the Bois de
Boulogne and the Avenue de Neuilly were
still crowded with fashionable equipages; and
the minister of public instruction was giving
away the prizes, the laurel crown, and the
kisses on both cheeks, to the tight-buttoned
pupils of the colleges. High festival was being

held at Dieppe, at Ostend, at Dunkirk. The
season was just beginning at Baden-Baden;
and the Jews of Hamburg were flocking over
to the queer little island of Heligoland — that
eccentric dependency of the British Crown,
which it possesses nobody knows how, and
nobody knows why — to eat large oysters and
gamble at the *trente et quarante* tables. In
three-fourths of habitable Europe the first of
September was sunny, joyous, balmy; but in
London the clerk of the weather ordered it
otherwise. He bade the slave of his caprice,
the great metropolis, lay aside her holiday robe
of gauze and golden tissue; he tore the summer
flowers from her *coiffure*, and commanded her
to attire herself all in dingy shivering gray.
It was warm on the sunny side of the way
even in Stockholm and Copenhagen that year;
but London was condemned to a sinister chilli-
ness, akin only to that felt in the great shivery-
shakery city of Petersburg, when, the first
fifteen days of August past, they light the gas
on the Nevskoi, and begin to cram the stoves
with charcoal; while careful housewives look

to the state of their double windows and to the listing of their doors; and moody bachelors examine what ravages the summer moths have made in their fur pelisses.

It blew great guns all day long, and the streets were nearly as empty as on a Derby day. People with goloshes, stout overcoats, and serviceable umbrellas — their own or borrowed — can stand rain. Some like it: I do. Furs, comforters, flannels, and woollen muffatees will keep out the cold: and hot brandy-and-water, when you can get enough of it, is a great crutch. In hot weather the philosopher can walk in a straw hat and his shirtsleeves; or, if he chooses to sacrifice to the graces, he may carry his coat genteelly over his arm. But you can't do anything with or against a windy day. *Omnia vincit amor.* So does the wind vanquish most things. It gets down your back; it insinuates itself between the flesh and the wristband of the tightest-buttoned glove; it draws tears from the eyes and rheum from the corners of the mouth; it makes the hair a torment and the cavities of the ears miseries; it causeth the teeth to chatter, and the lower garments to flap in an unseemly manner against the benumbed calves; it makes the nose to ache, and the bristles of the newly-shaven beard to tingle, and evoketh crimson blotches, unsightly to the eye, on the check-bones; it tyeth knots in ladies' cap ribbons, and bloweth their bonnets nine-bauble square, and sendeth hats away skimming, far away from human heads, baffling pursuit, injuring valuable property (the intrinsic value of a hat is immense, for it is the most difficult article in the whole wardrobe to obtain on credit), to the despair of the owners and the boisterous merriment of vulgar boys; it sendeth pungent dust up inflated nostrils, I hate the wind. It is a stupid leveller and irrational democrat; a ruffianly swaggerer, wrecking ships, smashing the roof of the Crystal Palace, tearing the limbs off good old oaks, tumbling over established chimney-pots, and weathercocks hallowed by time, making doors and windows to creak, howling in an unearthly and doggish manner, and exposing female ancles that should not be seen. I hate the wind; it is a fool—grinding corn for it knows not whom, and inflating the lungs of other fools to blow their own trumpets withal. I hate the wind for its levity; it is the lightest thing in the world, except a woman.

This bad wind had howled, and crooned, and whistled, and screeched, and gone on anyhow all day, playing the very deuce among the poles for drying linen in back gardens, making nurserymen at Battersea and Fulham clinch their fists, and mutter direful oaths as they surveyed their menaced hot-houses and cucumber frames, and generally trying people's tempers, and disturbing do-mestic felicity. Cabin-boys had a bad time of it that first of September, when the master of the collier came on board, after dinner, full of salt beef and new rum, and with his terrible "Colt" in his hand. Pinched child-ren, with harsh stepmothers, had reason to rue that windy day. Apprentices were sore harassed by the working jewellers, their masters, and meditated fleeing from their indentures to islands were watches grew on trees, and garnet brooches ran wild. Streets that had hitherto been hopelessly dirty were blown quite clean by the searching blast. Fallen leaves from the trees in St. James's Park were found high up in St. Martin's Lane, Holborn-wards. Beggars struggled up the streets under a press of tatters, and were compelled ever and anon to take in a reef in their rags. The patient cabhorses at the ranks bent their meek heads, and took refuge in well-sown nose-bags, where wind could not penetrate. The Jehus, their masters, crouched in rickety coffee-shops, into which the wind eddied fearfully, and blew their decoctions of burnt beans into brown ripples. The policeman had donned his oilskin cape, though it rained not, and the garment flapped and crackled like a dry leaf. Pipes would not keep alight, candles would not light at all, and if the sacred fire of Zoroaster had been kindled in Trafalgar Square, it would have gone out there and then.

The old Tower stood the brunt of the blast bravely, though the masts of the ships in the river bent like whips. The bridges were firm; but that of Hungerford, which they had been trying to build for some half dozen years or so, creaked and moaned dismally in its timber frame-work. It should have been dark at three, so wretched a day was it; but it kept grayly light till seven, when shuddering gas-lights began to wink and flicker in, as the sly wind insinuated itself through the crevices of the lamp-frames.

It struck seven by the clock of St. Mary-le-Strand as a wretched, ragged, forlorn man in middle life, by age—at the very bottom of life's ladder in misery—passed through the Wellington Street turnstile of Waterloo Bridge, and began to toil over towards the Surrey side.

He was unshorn, dirty and dishevelled, fierce and haggard to look upon; but his fierceness and haggardness were those of want, not crime. He wore a cloak—strange that not-to-be-eradicated propensity of pau-

perised men to wear cloaks—but the mantle
was one rag. You had better not ask me
whether his battered napless hat had either
crown or brim. My own private conviction
is that it had neither; but I don't wish to
exaggerate matters. Twisted round it, at
any rate, and, I believe, pinned with one
black pin and a white one, was a wisp of
gummy rusty crape : you know—that deadly
looking crape which forms the trimming to
the scant mantles of the old women in the
free seats of the parish church, who hustle
each other for the lees of the sacramental
wine, when the " miserable sinners " who are
better off have finished kneeling on the red
velvet hassocks round the altar rails, and
have departed in their carriages. He wore
this crape hat-rag—hat-band if you will—for
a little child of his that had died six months
before. He had another child at home who
was dying.

I don't want to be questioned about his
linen. I hope he had a shirt, but appearances were against him; and his coat was

buttoned up very high. When I say buttoned up, I may, I hope, be taken to mean
pinned up, sewn up, tied up, pasted up, glued
up, closed somehow tightly across his breast,
as it was. His boots were such prodigies
of bankruptcy and distress, that I must
refrain from describing them. The whole
man was such a walking tatter, that had
there been any charitable souls abroad that
windy day, there might have been haply some
pennies thrown at him, but for a miserable
compromise he had essayed to make between
utter present beggary and bygone respect-
ability. *He wore gloves!* Such gloves! such
woe-begone hand-slippers of faded Berlin of
some indescribable colour, if colour they had
ever possessed, bursting in holes all over,
through which the starved flesh showed itself
in discoloured patches, like unwholesome
blossoms.

This man, battling with the unkind breeze,
which blew due east from Shoreditch Railway Station, and beyond that from the
bleak headlands of Suffolk, might have been

a begging-letter imposter, elaborately "got up" to represent a reduced gentleman, or a decayed tradesman. He might have been a destitute Polish refugee, or a professor of languages with no pupils, or a man with a Chancery suit, or a discoverer of perpetual motion, or one of the fifty thousand castaways with more brains than bread, who are for ever wandering in this metropolis, and whom, if they were set in the pillory, it would be a mercy to pelt with hard-boiled eggs, so that they might eat them afterwards.

He was none of these, but our old friend Philip Leslie, six-and-thirty years of age, quite ruined, broken, and hopeless. Time had dealt no more hardly with him than she had done by thousands of better men, who had been in greater straits, who had suffered greater agonies, who had deserved richer rewards, and who, in one instance only, had been treated with a mercy as yet denied him: in being permitted to Die. He had worked, but nothing had come of it; studied, but nothing had come of it; toiled and striven,

but nothing had come of it—save this: The
rags, a sick wife at home, a dying child.
His *kismet*, his fate, was against him. He
had no luck. Such things happen every
day.

I will endeavour to relate his sorry history,
since you last parted from him, in a very
few words. You have guessed already—I
need scarcely tell you again—that it was by
Philip Leslie's hand that Charles Falcon, Lord
Baddington, fell in the wood of Vincennes,
the morning after the *bal masqué*. I have
never been able to ascertain with any degree
of certainty, how Philip managed to effect
his escape, which he did quite uninterrupted
and unmolested immediately after the duel;
but I have no doubt he was indebted for
his safety to the good offices of the ubiqui-
tous Doctor Ionides, who, Philip noticed,
seemed to be on the very best terms with the
French police, as far as regarded smoothing
away passport difficulties, and answering
embarrassing questions. But though the
Doctor, or the Professor, or the Captain, or

Jack Pollyblank in fact, behaved in the kindest manner to him, "like a Dutch uncle," as he himself humorously expressed it, in bringing him off scot free from the consequences of his deadly encounter, and landing him safe and sound in the fairy mansion in Curzon Street, and in the presence of his lady patroness, Philip could by no means prevail upon him to keep another promise which he had made him, and with some degree of solemnity. Neither entreaties nor remonstrances could move him to redeem his pledge of giving Philip good news of Manuelita, the dancing-girl, or to disclose her whereabouts. He persisted in gloomily averring that he knew nothing of the "hussey"; and after Philip had challenged him to fight another duel—having, like the tiger, gotten an appetite for blood with the first taste—at which cartel he was immensely amused, but jocosely declined it; telling Philip in good-humoured confidence, that if he attempted to have recourse to such personal violence as he might deem would force him to demand

personal satisfaction, he would feel himself
called upon to break his jaw, jump on his
ribs—"mark him so that his mother wouldn't
know him," was the Doctor's amicable de-
finition of the operation—choosing a secluded
spot for the performance of the feat. Philip
Leslie thought the wisest thing he could
do was to leave the depraved giant to his own
devices, and to abandon the hopeless pursuit.
He revolved all the chances of the matter
in his mind; but was unable to decide as to
whether Pollyblank had sequestered Manuelita
for his own purposes, or whether he was kept
from her by order of Lady Baddington.
Both the man and the woman were inscrutable beings to him, and he had neither
patience enough, nor moral courage nor will
enough, to probe the subject further.

"Had he ever loved Manuelita?" I leave
you divine. Throughout these hazy pages—
these sheets written in danger and distress, in
sickness and contumely — commenced in a
darkened room surrounded by the shadows
of death, and drawing rapidly to a limping

termination now in a strange land, far away from the friends I love and the kinsfolk who love me not—I have never dared to decide *myself* what were the real motives, the thoughts in the holy of holies of the hearts of the people whose shadowy likenesses I have drawn. I have endeavoured, so far as my lights will permit me, to tell you what they thought and felt; but there are secrets in their souls I cannot fathom. For all shadowy as they are, and rudely and clumsily depicted, I Believe in my people. They are not puppets, they are not marionettes; they are not stocks and stones. They exist. They do. They would walk and talk, they would live and breathe, if a more cunning hand than mine could lift the curtain that veils them. I know Jack Pollyblank. I have seen Tinctop. I have dined with Lord Baddington, the old one and the young one. I have been in love with Généviève; I, who write. But my diction is incoherent, and my speech is thick and clogged, like that of a dumb man who has been but half reclaimed from mutism by the care of a learned professor. I can see the shapely statue, I can appreciate the glowing picture; but my fingers are clumsy, and cannot mould; my hand is false to my eye, and will not colour.

Did Philip love Manuelita, and so easily resign her? I tell you that question is not one easily to be decided, or without a more searching perception than falls to the lot of most men. I hate such fools, who jump at such conclusions hastily.

For some time after the return of Philip Leslie to England, his lines fell into pleasant places, and he prospered exceedingly. The Lady Baddington was good enough to introduce him into society. He gave drawing lessons, at a guinea a *séance*, to some of the highest families of the aristocracy. His manner was spoken of, by dowagers almost ineffable in their rank and wealth, as being *distingué*. It was about this time that he knew several lords. His pictures sold well. He had plenty of commissions. The Marquis Tarradiddle talked of sending him to Rome to

make water-colour drawings of the arabesques
in the *loggie* and *stanze* of the Vatican. He
spent a whole month at Loavesandfishes, the
charming retreat, in the New Forest, of the
Lord Bishop of Bosfursus. He had the
grandes and the *petites entrées* in Curzon
Street; and her Ladyship was always kind
and gracious to him. He lived in handsome
apartments in George Street, Hanover Square;
rode a horse in the park; was on the can-
didates' list for the Praxiteles Club; and
saved five hundred pounds.

His fortune, you will say, was made; but
what do you think this ungrateful, infatuated
young man did? He went and married Lucy
Stevens, the governess to the Lord Bishop
Bosfursus's daughter, a pale-faced young
creature, not yet eighteen, and without a
penny to bless herself with.

CHAP. XLVIII.

WHITHER TEND THE CROOKED ROADS.

SPEED thee onward, ragged man over the bridge, for there is death before thee and death behind thee. Speed thee onward over the bridge; for it is not good to halt in the bays or look through the balustrades. Speed thee onward.

And be thou accursed, bridge of the fear-some memories, for there is blood upon thy coping-stones, and thy parapets are wet with the tears of women. Never came there any good out of thee; nor profit to the money-spinners that built thee, nor health to those who from thy flagged footways inhaled the deadly miasma of the river; nor a whisper of solace to the wretched, nor of rest to the weary. The feet of the night-prowlers have worn smooth thy stones, and thy roadway has been rutted by the wheels of the chariots that drove fools to their folly and the froward to their destruction. Malison on thee, bridge, that see'st unmoved misery and despair, and the cracking of heartstrings; bridge, at whose toll-gates might stand Charon on the one side, and the dog Cerberus on the other; and o'er whose barriers might be written, as above the Inferno's doors, " Ye who enter, leave all hope behind."

The ragged man that was Philip Leslie struggled over the bridge, speeding him to-wards his miserable home. He had married the governess, and come to grief. As he had made his bed, so he must lie. If he would so fly in the face of his best friends, what could he expect? His best friends told him this, and a variety of other edifying things, when they discarded him. The Viscountess Bad-dington, in the few brief words in which she informed him that he was never more to expect countenance or assistance from her, took occasion to tell him that he was a mean, spirit-less fool. Good heaven! what had the man done? what was he to do? He wasn't a lord; why should'nt he marry the governess? But it was agreed on all sides that he committed an act of gross folly, imprudence, and in-gratitude. There is a wonderful unanimity sometimes among people when the fugleman is powerful; and aristocratic England un-animously sent Philip Leslie to Coventry: those who had ordered pictures countermanded them; and some even who had received the works for which they had given commissions were so indignant at the hideous turpitude dis-played by Philip in forming that unfortunate matrimonial alliance with the governess, that they would have no more to do with him on any account—not even to the extent of paying him what they owed him. Philip went to law with one quondam patron, the Marquis of Gumbo, author of the Gumbo overcoat and the Gumbo mail-phaeton. His butler called to pay the money a few days after Philip had been bold enough to issue a writ; and the next day Mr. Fusbos, of Regent Street, the great picture-dealer, and extensively patronised by Lord Gumbo, refused to buy any more of Philip's pictures at any price.

Genius accompanied by industry, however it may have to encounter adversity in the outset, must ever, you may say, triumph in the long run? Must it! I tell you that against some men there *is* this *kismet*, this adverse fate; that against them there has gone forth a fiat of ill-luck, and that whether the wheel of fortune move swiftly or slowly, up-hill, or down-hill, still, crushed beneath the tire, at the bottommost spoke of the wheel, will those men be. They tried a man for vagabondage in France, the other day, before some tribunal of correctional police. They found, on removing his cap, tattooed on his forehead, this strange inscription—"*Pas de chance.*" He had never had a chance. He never was to have one. If he had painted like Raphael, or sung like Tasso, there was yet to be "no luck" about that miserable human house of his. These

Murads the Unlucky, these John Hardups, must always exist, I suppose, in order to preserve the equal balance of society, teach us our duties, the value of contentment, the futility of vain efforts, and much more in the didactic and generally imbecile department.

So, after his little brief season of prosperity, "swift as an arrow from a Tartar's bow" went Philip Leslie to ruin. The fuglewoman of his chorus of detractors was powerful, able, merciless. He fell into the hands of small picture-dealers and disreputable furniture brokers. His works figured at low auction-rooms in Drury Lane and on Holborn Hill. Then he began to work for the Jews; then having pawned everything to buy bread, he took to selling tickets to buy drink. He was kind enough to, and fond enough of, the poor, feeble, sickly girl he had married: only they were too poor to be fond of one another. I have heard of love in a cottage, and believed in it. I have tried, myself, love in a back kitchen, and have found a cooking-range and a mangle things not wholly insupportable.

Were it not for the black beetles, I should prefer it to love in marble halls.   But love in a second floor back; love in one room, with the bed in the corner, the whole place in a perpetual state of babytude, with a little pile of pawn tickets on the mantelpiece, with the landlady coming up every ten minutes to tell you, in acrid accents, that her landlord will call for his rent to-morrow, so that she will trouble you to settle your little account to-day; love with no coals in the grate, and none in the cupboard, my dear, loses much of its poesy—becomes, in fact, something very like horrible, soul-grinding, heartbreaking prose.

They had a baby or two born in due course, but death had mercifully cut down the little daisies in their meadow till within some eighteen months of the time at which I found Philip again for you.   Baby the last lived, a rickety, suffering, feeble little Christian; a poor, white thing, with large eyes that kept ever regarding you—ah! so wistfully, ah! so sadly, as though to ask if this squalid misery, this pinching penury of second-floor-existence, were the most notable features in the fine showy thing called Life, that men make such fuss about. This was the baby that was ill; and, with its mother, lay on a bed in the corner of a back-room lodging, meekly, uncomplainingly waiting for death.

He had reached home at last, the ragged man. Home had its habitat in a street turning out of the Waterloo Road—a street that I may be excused for calling one-eyed, for it had houses and windows only on one side; the length of the other being entirely occupied by the high brick dead wall of a thundering minor theatre, the Royal Guelph and Ghibelline Theatre, if I am not mistaken. A flaming placard of many colours, nearly as long as the wall itself was pasted on it, very high up, and out of the reach of filibustering billstickers of rival establishments. It informed the world that the Royal G. G. Theatre was unrivalled. That it was the Home of the Drama. That it was the favourite resort of the nobility and gentry, and that it was favoured with continual over-flows and an unprecedented succession of bril-

liant novelties. References were made to the
startling melodrama of "Leary Jem; or the
Life Preserver and the Lagged One;" also to
the forthcoming real old Surrey side domestic
drama, "Smiles and Tears; or, the Union, the
Mill, the Jug, and the Stepper." Talma
Coggs, the great Transpontine comedian,
known among his admirers in the New Cut as
"Speak-out Coggs," had been engaged at an
immense sacrifice to perform the part of Leary
Jem for six nights longer at this temple of the
drama.   Philip had vainly tried to obtain
employment in his old 'vocation of a scene-
painter. They had taken him on for about a
fortnight one Christmas-time to foil-paper-up
some coral columns in the grand transforma-
tion scene of the pantomime—the dazzling
halls of enchanting delight in the realms of
of Rumtyidity; but the curse of the Viscountess's anger seemed to pursue him everywhere. The management contemptuously re-
corded its opinion that "there was no good in
that fellow;" he drank, he smoked, he was
always playing cribbage, he neglected his wife

he didn't wash, he wasn't clever; he was lazy, proud, conceited, unprincipled, they said. Hundreds of things were said of the same sort; for, you see, the world was against him. Terrible odds, those: yourself against the world!

He had been out all the morning, trying to borrow, or beg, or get a little money anyhow. They had physic from the dispensary in sufficient quantity; but there are times when the best dose of physic is a bottle of port wine, and the best bolus a beefsteak. But there was no money in London that windy day — none, at least, for Philip Leslie. There was such a tightness in the money-market, and about the entrance to the trouser's pockets of mankind — such a padlocking of human hearts, and hasping, barring, stapling, and chaining up of human sympathies — that Philip might as well have appealed to Alderman Waithman's obelisk at the corner of Fleet Street, or Charles the First's statue at Charing Cross, as to men and women that day. There was no money in the city (where things, by the way, had been

terribly bad lately), and no money in Westminster. The few friends who yet remained
to him were either too poor to assist, or tired
out by repeated loans to him. Misery to you
when you have worn out the kindness and
forbearance of your friends! How he had
succeeded in his interview with her Grace the
Duchess of Minniver, once Viscountess Baddington, you have already learnt through the
medium of Mr. Tinctop's mamma. He had
seen her Grace again that day — the day of
the wind — but not to speak to her. Her
luxurious chariot, the ducal coronet on
the panels, was rolling swiftly through
Oxford Street. He had just caught one
glimpse of her beautiful face, with her golden
hair shining and wavering amidst the lace of
her bonnet. He saw it all, for a moment.
The warm autumn dress, the tiny sable muff,
the Skye-terrier, sitting in supreme ugliness,
an animated ball of worsted in her lap. The
rosy coachman had five capes to his coat, and
wore a wig; the flour on the footman's head
would have made bread for the dear ones at

home; the trinkets about the small-veined
heads of the horses would have made the
second-floor back a palace; the very car-
riage-rug was ampler, warmer, than all the
bed-furniture he had, poor man, put together. And he, destitute, forlorn, castaway,
he had enjoyed all these things. He had sate
on the soft cushions, ridden in the carriage,
lain at the woman's feet, kissed her false hand,
been petted by her — beautiful, cruel, wicked,
as she was. It was all over, now — never to
return. Did you never look at a scene, a
thing, a face you had enjoyed, revelled in,
played with, caressed, and, revisiting it, or
seeing it pass, feel that there was a gulf ten
thousand miles wide between you and what
was once your goods and chattels — your
slave and plaything. So, looking, the voice of
your heart cries " Never more, never more!"
and you slowly and sadly plod on the way of all
men born to die. And so the carriage passed
Philip, and left him (with some of the mud
from its wheels on his torn clothes) in the
midst of Oxford Street, the opium eater's

"stony-hearted step-mother." The carriage
stopped at the door of the Pantheon, and the
Duchess alighted and entered the bazaar.
What was she doing in town, now that the
season was over? Why was she not on her
way to the Continent, to one of her princely
castles and palaces? With an insane, hopeless,
almost mechanical clinging to the phantom of
that which once has been, Philip followed the
carriage, and was about to enter the building;
but a sumptuous beadle, with a golden bulb,
like a pumpkin, at the top of his staff, drove
him back frowningly, making indignant comments on his torn apparel, and shapeless,
shameful boots. Oh! the unpardonable Sin of
Poverty! Miss Teazlum's school for young
ladies was just filing out of the bazaar as the
repulse took place. Clara Fisher, the belle of
the school, laughed. Laura Toogood, the wag
(a bold girl), made a face at the wretched man
as she passed him; but a sigh stole from little
Kitty Clover's lips, and she said, "Poor
fellow!" He did look very poor, indeed. But
for fear of Miss Teazlum, Kitty would have

run after the ragged man and given him that fourpenny-piece, the last remains of Uncle John's bright silver crown. As it was, a tear stood in her eye. She was always crying at other people's sorrows, and laughing at her own: this foolish little school-girl. God bless thee, little Kitty: pleasant little Samaritan, with soft brown hair plaited into two tails, the gipsy hat and the frilled trousers. God bless thee, though I met thee but once, and for a moment, in a crowded street. Go thy ways, and be happier than the wretched man whom thou didst pity.

Spurned from the door, ragged Philip had that afternoon prowled up Poland Street, and so into Great Marlborough Street, where you know is situated the back entrance to the Pantheon Bazaar. And as he passed the door, a man went in swiftly; a man with huge black whiskers, and dressed in a showy, flashy, half-foreign style. He was visible but for a moment, and was gone.

"As I live," cried Philip, "that must be Jack Pollyblank."

At other times, long, long ago, he had scornfully refused the fellow's proferred aid; but now he would have taken a crown, a shilling from him, and have been thankful for it.   He pressed quickly to the door, and would have entered; but he was repulsed again by a second edition of the sumptuous beadle, who told him, in no very polite terms, that the place was not for such as he.

" But I have a friend here, a gentleman, whom I must see," Philip said, vainly struggling to obtain admittance.

" A friend, a gentleman! I dessay," the official answered, sneeringly.   " A friend, I spose, who is fond of priggin things off the counters, and isn't at all awerse to the flower-pots in the conservatory.   Come, git along with you, or I'll call the 'plice."

There was nothing to be done, nothing to be said; and with a heart long since as heavy, but now growing harder than the nether mill-stone, Philip Leslie turned on his heels, and stalked gloomily down Carnaby Street.   There was mischief in the man.

So he had come home to the house in the slum, desperate, penniless, for his last halfpenny had gone to pay the bridge-toll. Somebody was walking with him, solitary as he seemed. The somebody was not Jack Pollyblank:—had the beadle not warned him off the Pantheon premises, that somebody would not have made his appearance, and all things in his life might have been changed. As it was, Somebody linked his arm in his. It was the same somebody who had been his companion along the great north road, as he sped on his two hundred and ten miles' journey to London, years before. The house in which was his miserable room had a shop attached to it, a chandler's-shop: a dank little glory-hole of a place. It made Philip doubly desperate to look at the eatables displayed in the window, cumbering the shelves and counter, coarse, rank viands at best; mouldy cheese, rancid butter, bacon, red herrings, saveloys, and loaves of inferior bread. Coarse as they were, they would have been luxuries to him; but his credit had long since been exhausted. He was in debt for victuals and in debt for rent, and not one penny more in cash or kind could he raise.

"I can't go in," he muttered, stopping on the threshold of the door; "I can't go in; God help me." And burst out crying.

It was not good to see him cry. I tell you that there was mischief in him. His were not the tears of a tender sorrow that in weeping finds relief, but tears rather of burning impatience and rage against the world that had been so hard upon him; against the men and women who had used him so cruelly. Those tears were the salt waves of the Black Sea of Despair. He repeated again to himself that he could not go in yet, and that he would take a little walk. Then slunk up the street into the Waterloo Road again.

Oh rash and miserable man, pause and come back! The golden prime is come: wealth, honours, titles, await thee in the wretched two-pair back. There, demurely sitting by thy sick wife's side is Seth Tinctop, hiding the Levite beneath the Samaritan's robe, and for once pouring oil and balm into her wounds. There is a flush upon her pallid cheek, as he tells her that thou art a peer of the realm — a lord of the land — that thou wilt have vast estates, and stores of gold, and silver, and jewels. There is a viscount's coronet (with a slight law-suit attached to it, whose expenses Mr. Tinctop will gladly pay) waiting for thee upstairs.

Pause, then—nay, speed thee onward if the inexorable fates have willed it so. The curse of blood-guiltiness is upon thee, and never came happiness yet from that title of Baddington. So he went onward, and the shadows of the evening closed up behind him like drapery, as he plunged into the maze of streets.

CHAP. XLIX.

SHADOWS.

THE Christmas bells ring cheerily across the lea as I pen these lines; and carts laden with misletoe and holly, sparkling and blushing with their crimson and milkwhite berries — the rubies and pearls of Flora's inexhaustible jewel casket — the horses come plodding into the frozen town, bowing their heads as though they strove to melt the icy ruts with the hot blue breath that curls from their nostrils; the carters, pipe in mouth, and their hands ill defended by worsted mits, tucked beneath their smock-frocks, jog by the sides of the Christmas chariots. The chubby children, with winter

roses in their cheeks for bloom, and tears
of joy for Christmas that is coming trembling
in their eye-corners (for I will not have it
said, that the tears shed for Christmas' sake
can ever be sorrowful), follow the bough-
cumbered cart with much hand-clapping and
shrill hurraying, picking up, by times, stray
sprigs of evergreen, or begging from good-
humoured guardians, the earliest morsels of
misletoe, with which, incontinent, they make
themselves brave, and sow pleasant tumult
and disorder in the breasts of little maidens,
aged eight, by precocious accolades of the
most Archi-druidical character. Now do the
jagged streets of country boroughs become
immoderately gay; now bow-windows, sacred
during the rest of the year to the whitest
of dimity curtains (with that peculiar, fluffy,
cottony, bed-furniture trimming, which only
country housekeepers seem to know how to
knit) windows enlivened only by plants belonging to the severer sections of the Lin-
næan system, and cages full of canary-birds,
whose choristry is so decorous, whose bearing

is so demure (they never put their heads aggressively on one side, nor peck turbulently at the sugar-lumps, like some feathered roysterers I know) that you might fancy they were trilling hymns, and were, themselves, dissenting dicky-birds: now do these ordinarily staid and composed casements, with panes so bright that the bellman, as he cries the lost or stolen puppy-dog, can see his red face reflected in the *carreaux ;* that the curate settles his white neckcloth by their aid as he passes, and the two Miss Flosses give their auburn ringlets a corkscrew twist of arrangement, with those *impromptu* mirrors' assistance: — now do the gleaming but sober windows, through which the calm countenances are visible, of starch-capped old ladies, busy over lamb's-wool knitting, or killing the sunny hours with such light literature as " Bogatsky's Golden Treasury," or good Doctor Buchan's " Domestic Medicine: " windows that sometimes display the bald heads, brass buttons, and ample waistcoats of the fathers of families, and sometimes the

wicked, impish visage of that animal I loathe
chiefly among living creatures — a cat —
slily watching the canary-birds, and indulging
with Jesuitical patience and pertinacity, for
months and months together, in the pursuit
of unlicensed game under difficulties; and
sometimes the broad, ruddy, shiny face of a
housemaid, rather bored and dull when the
family are from home: a placid Mariana,
in an unmoated grange, and aweary, aweary
at the perfidy of the journeyman baker who
cometh not, she says, and wishing devoutly,
not that she were dead — she enjoys her life
too thoroughly, the cheery lass! — but that
she were married to a corporal of the
Sappers and Miners: now, for the last time,
do these WINDOWS blaze forth in leaved and
berried splendour. Now shall you see ruddy
reflections (from the great fire whereon the
chestnuts roast) on the ceiling within. Now,
if your ears be sharp enough, may you hear
the click of knives and forks, and the cheery
jingle of young voices; and now, at the
windows themselves, may you see the clus-

tering vines of happy children's faces, and the blooming fig-trees of innumerable pretty female cousins, and other joys and delights of Home, that make me sad to think about. Lo Christmas is here, and all the Universe is glad.

And I sit before the murky wood-fire in the bare gaunt room, in the strange land far away, the bellows on my knees, vainly blowing to provoke a few Christmas sparks from that grey smouldering log. But the bellows' nozzle is rebellious, and the leathern-stomached wooden-sided fire-compeller will give no freshening blow, but only an asthmatic wheeze, so I fling the bellows pettishly away; they fall upon the red-tiled floor, and a resident echo jars my heartstrings. I draw down the iron-veil of the fire-place, and rake together the scattered embers; but the fire will not draw, and only a dull, murky smoke begins to billow forth, and circles round my bed. It is twilight in the street at four o'clock, this dismal, alien Christmas time, and the room is full of shadows.

Shadows of the real, shadows of the un-real — shadows of what has been, and never will be again; shadows of what has never been, and never can come to pass. They commingle and blend duskily; they are trans-muted; light gleams for an instant through the crepuscule and darker shadows roll, and are for ever rolling. Dim shapes loom faintly in the maze, wild shapes, indistinct shapes, and yet from time to time they bear a mo-mentary semblance to the people who have flitted across this tremulous panorama of mine. Now I seem to know them well, and clutch at their individualities. Généviève, Manuelita, Philip, Tinctop, Pollyblank, the dead father Falcon, the dead woman, in her first bright beauty in the Kentish village: they are all here: and now the shadows vanquish me again, and there is darkness.

A meteoric gleam lights up the troubled field of view, and shows me a wretched chandler's shop in a shabby street, hard by the Waterloo Road. The house is full of weeping and wailing and bitter lamentations.

In a second-floor back-room there is a sick woman with a sick child and a knot of gossipping harridans — chattering, magging crones — who try to console the invalid in her dire affliction. And sore need has she of consolation, poor soul! For downstairs, in the shabby street, there are Bearers — bearers with a dreadful burden. It is in a species of long and hideous palanquin, placed on a stretcher. It is covered with some coarse black drapery. It is girt about with ropes and straps, and, with its shrouded mystery, freezes and appals. See here: the woman in the back-room had a husband, one Philip Leslie by name, they say — a forlorn man who painted scenes for the theatre. He went out early two days ago, and returned not. Now he is come back. Recognised by a police-constable who knew him well by sight when living, he was brought from the place where they found him, in the river's slimy ooze — blue and bruised, in the mud, among the rotting timber, and the river's ghastly logs. They have brought his dreadful

dead body home — drowned. What good can
there be in bringing him here? Take him
away for pity's sake, to the pauper dead-
house. Here are no shrouds to enwrap him,
no biers to coffin him, nothing but a wretched,
sickly woman to sob over him, while a feeble
infant wails. Take him away, and bid the
beadle apprise the coroner (who will not dine
at Kensington Gore to day, but will spend
his evening at a lowering little public-house
in Lambeth Marsh) and summon the jury for
the inquest.

Now with eager but unsteady hands, I try
to tear the veil away, and seek to dispel
the shadows that gather over the Future of
the woman and the child. With ear, in which
heart-pulses beat, I listen, and still listen for
tidings of Tinctop. I burn to know how he
has sped in his mission to restore the coronet
to the rightful heir. All the magging crones
are busy, telling the widow that her baby is a
Lord. Ah! I hear something, but not from
her, not from them. The landlady of the
chandler's shop tells one of *her* gossips that

the nice-spoken gentleman who was " drove " in his brougham, who came to see Mrs. Leslie two days since, and waited to see her husband, and who left a sovereign with her as he went away, promised to return the next day. But he has not been back.

" P'raps he don't mean to come again," says the chandler's shopkeeper.

" P'raps something's happened to him," suggests the gossip.

Why should anything happen to so nicely-spoken a gentleman, and one besides, driven in his own brougham, as was Mr. Tinctop?

I want to know more about that sick woman and her child; but the shadows are obstinate, and the voices are mute. It is impossible that the woman and child can live. They are *so* ill, so weak, so destitute, so unhappy. I wait and wait for Tinctop to return, and for his elaborate plot to be at length unravelled; for his scheme of vengeance against Généviève, sometime Viscountess Baddington, to be at length brought to consummation. Now I strain my eyes to pierce the shadows' gloomiest

gulfs, and seem to discern a crowded court-
room in which an action of ejectment is being
tried before the judges of the land. I listen
to the arguments for Philip Falcon, falsely
called Leslie, and claiming to be Viscount
Baddington in the peerage of Great Britain
and Ireland, by his next friend. Who is his
next friend, I wonder? — against the Duke
and Duchess of Minniver. Sergeant Supple
will be for the plaintiff; Mr. Lingolong, Q.C.,
for the defendants. There will be paragraphs
in the Sunday newspapers about the case,
headed " Romance in High Life." What excitement there will be, when the Duke and
Duchess have to disgorge £10,000 a-year, and
the little boy is legally proved to be heir to
such a princely income! Surely Tinctop will
be triumphant. Then will come the great
Baddington Peerage case before the Committee
of Privileges of the House of Lords. Supple
and Lingolong, with cohorts of junior counsel,
are at it again, tooth and nail. I seem to hear
their specious arguments *pro* and *con*, their
glib, oily voices, the rustle of their silk robes,

the yawns of the grey-headed law lords as they fidget on their crimson benches. But ah! the pall of shadows falls over the deceptive picture; and in a mist I seem to see a fleeting image of a green churchyard and a new-made grave.

Before Heaven, this is no shadow, but an awful Reality. I see two men in earnest confabulation together in the back-parlour of a shop full of extraordinary odds and ends, and rags, and rich dresses, in Windmill Street, Tottenham Court Road. One of the men is bald and shiny headed, is sleek in face and sleek in apparel, and has a quiet, cat-like appearance in his gestures. The other is a big, stout man, with huge black whiskers and a loud coarse voice. He is dressed in a showy, flashy, half-foreign style, and swears a good deal when he talks. The sleek bald-headed man calls him Jack, and presses pipes and spirits on him; but he seems very uneasy in his presence, nevertheless, and continually wishes that his mother would come home. But the individual addressed as Jack tells him that he needn't worry himself, for that Mrs.

Tinctop is not coming home just yet, admitting, indeed, having resorted to a pious fraud in keeping her out of the way, wishing to have some quiet and confidential conversation with his dear friend Tinctop. He and his dear friend Tinctop talk long and eagerly: their voices are somewhat sharply pitched. They use high words. I am afraid they are going to quarrel. Heavens and earth! what was that? A blow. The whiskered man has felled his dear friend Tinctop, and has him on the encumbered floor, his fingers on his throat, his knee on his chest.

I hear the wretched man who is undermost ejaculate something like a prayer for mercy.

"You wretched half-bred fox-cub you," the whiskered man replied savagely, "I'll warm your cockles for you, you mangy rat."

"Mercy!" Tinctop again moans.

"*Connais pas*," the whiskered man returns, tightening his grasp. "If it was my game to spare you, 1 would. What is a man's life to me! Bah! that."

He taps the nail of his forefinger contemp-

tuously against his front tooth. I hear the
sharp click now. The victim takes advantage
of this movement to endeavour to release himself, and to raise a cry for help; but his foe
had his knee on his chest and his throat in his
grip. There is a hideous, hellish struggle.
Then two blows with something blunt, a
piercing shriek, a faint moan, a gush of a
crimson fountain, and then a great bloody
snake begins to wind and welter along the
floor among the odds and ends.

"And now," says Mr. Jack Pollyblank,
rising from the corpse and shaking himself,
"I hope you're satisfied, my Lady Duchess."

The shadows are blacker than ever. Blacker,
blacker. But now suddenly lighted up by a
great conflagration. The ladies' wardrobe
shop in Windmill Street is burnt to the
ground. The charred trunk of Mr. Tinctop
is found, scarcely recognisable, in the back
parlour. There is a coroner's inquest. Adjourned inquiry. There are additional particulars and latest details. There is a verdict:
Accidental Death.

At least, if human justice be not dead and buried for ever, there should be another picture among the shadows. I should see that grim prison of Newgate whither a Lord of Baddington went once to visit a prisoner accused of forgery, and returning thence was stunned, and, after lingering a little while, died. I should see a man in a condemned cell, into whose deaf ears the ordinary pours hopeless messages of hope, and who — the callous ruffian — when the Sheriffs ask him if he has any last request to make, answers that he is much obliged, and that he would like a beefsteak and onions—shredded fine—for his breakfast on Monday morning. I should see that Monday morning, the crowds surging against the barriers, the windows of the houses alive with anxious human faces; I should hear the bell of St. Sepulchre's tolling, and the horrid yell that greets the man—the murderer, John Pollyblank—as he comes forth by the debtors' door to be hanged by the neck until he is dead. I should see the white cap drawn over his face, sneering and defiant to the last; I should see the halter adjusted and the drop fall; but there are no such things among the shadows. Not that the Pollyblank face disappears entirely from my vision. He is visible in an odd, furtive, masquerading manner. A form like Pollyblank's goes backwards and forwards, and wanders up and down in many and various costumes, the owner always well provided with money. Here is the Sovereign of a vast empire come to visit a brother potentate. She lands at Boulogne, on her way to Paris. She is received with cannon and shouting, and trumpeting and drumming, and banner-waving. She passes from her yacht to the quay, and along a richly-piled carpet to the railway-station. A lane is formed by two lines of bowing, liveried, decorated officials. Who is that portly gentleman, slightly bald, irreproachably white-cravated, and with the ribbon of the Legion of Honour—yes, of Honour—at his button-hole. He bows the lowest, he smiles the silkiest, as the Queen of England passes. Is he a chamberlain, a secretary of legation, a departmental prefect?

Anon I see him again, in Paris, but in a blouse and a fur cap, and wearing a huge red beard, swaggering about the Boulevards, and yelling, " *Vive l'Empereur! Vive la Reine!*" as a royal and imperial *cortège* passes. I see him again when a great crime is being attempted in the Rue Lepelletier, opposite the Grand Opera, and a carriage is riddled, and an Emperor's hat is grazed, and scores of un-offending men and women are torn to death by fragments of shells that have been cast upon the roadway, filled with fulminating mercury. Our portly friend, in full evening dress this time, and with a crush hat under his arm, is very busy on the occasion, and is even slightly wounded in the elbow by a splinter. Henceforth he carries his arm in a sling, and wears an extra ribbon, even as a veteran of Napoleon's grand army. I see him again at a trial in the English central criminal court. A great political prosecution, affecting the life of an exile, is going on. This time our stout friend, who is a material witness for the crown, is profoundly ignorant of English. He is examined through an interpreter. His name is the Chevalier de la Poulemouillée, and he listens, with a puzzled air, admirably assumed, to the fervent oration of Mr. Edwin James. And the last I see and hear of our stout friend among the shadows is at another trial, a political prosecution also, but in France. Again he is examined for the crown, and deposes to having followed about and watched the prisoner for months, and made notes of actions and conversation. The counsel for the defence elicits from him that he has gone under many different aliases. "Bah!" testily retorts the Procureur Impérial, settling his *toque* on his head, and looking contemptuously at the inexperienced young advocate for the defence, " *Qu'est-ce-que cela fait?* Judas, Vidocq, Vautrin, Delahodde, Jachimo, Ionides, Pollyblank — what does it matter?" The honourable President knows *de qui ce Monsieur relève*, who are his employers, and whence he comes. The honourable President nods his head in acquiescence; the honourable witness grins; the young advocate for the defence blushes and is silent; the Procureur Impérial sums up in a *chalereuse allocution*, and the prisoner is found guilty. If the shadows do not deceive me, the honourable witness comes from the Rue de Jérusalem, and is a spy of the secret police.

The shadows tell me no more; but I have eyes of my own, and can see things as well as most people. I saw her Grace the Duchess of Minniver looking more beautiful than ever, though she is past thirty now, at the Handel Festival, at the Crystal Palace. Her entertainments are also grander than ever; and they say that she is to be the next Mistress of the Robes. She has no children. She is a Puseyite of the most advanced category; and her piety and benevolence are in everybody's mouth. As for Mademoiselle Manuelita, she is a *première danseuse* at the San Carlo at Naples, and is much protected by the Russian legation. *On dit*, that the secretary, Count

Coatoff, is wild after her. They have offered her twenty thousand roubles for a three months' season in St. Petersburg. Somebody might meet her there again some day.

THE END.